ExPLORING THE ICE AGE

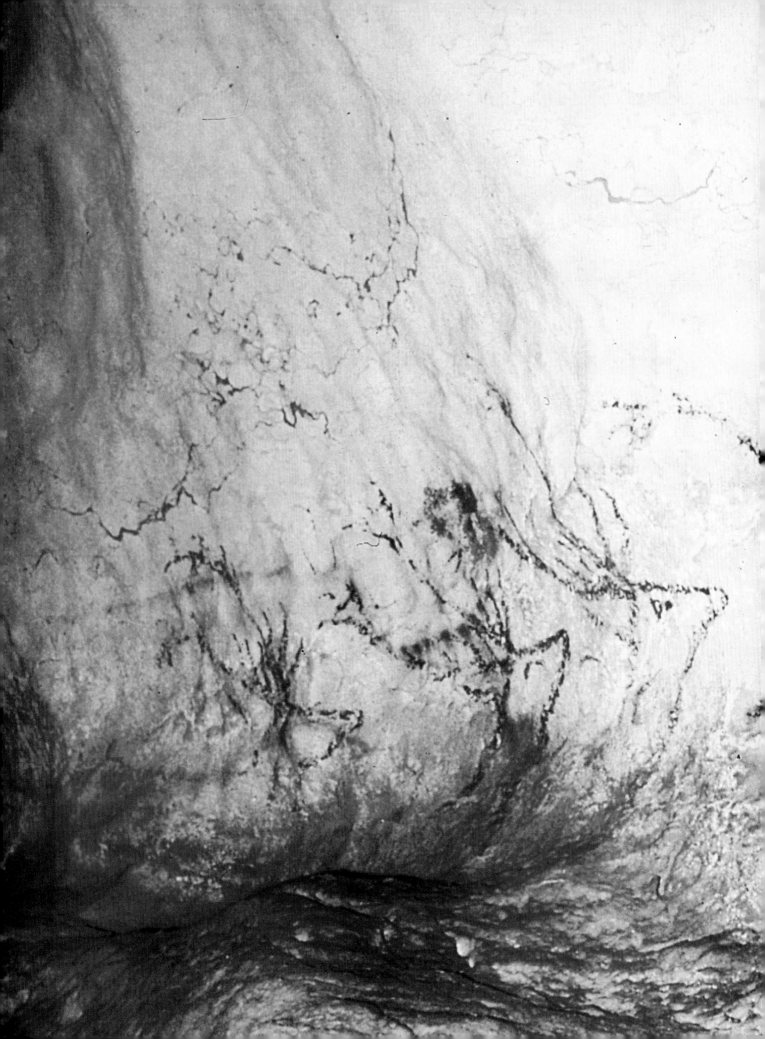

Exploring the Ice Age

By Margaret Cooper

Atheneum Books for Young Readers

New York London Toronto Sydney Singapore

For
Barbara and Harold,
Elaine and Alex
fellow travelers to the Ice Age

Atheneum Books for Young Readers
An imprint of Simon & Schuster Children's Publishing Division
1230 Avenue of the Americas
New York, New York 10020

Text copyright © 2001 by Margaret Cooper

Book design by Edward Miller

The text of this book is set in Bembo

Printed in the United States of America

10 9 8 7 6 5 4 3 2 1

Library of Congress Cataloging-in-Publication Data
Cooper, Margaret.
Exploring the ice age / by Margaret Cooper.—1st ed.
p.   cm.
Includes bibliographical references and index.
Summary: Describes the lives of those dwelling in Europe during the Ice Age and
discusses how they survived the harsh conditions of that period.
ISBN 0-689-82556-0
1. Paleolithic period—Europe—Juvenile literature. 2. Glacial epoch—Europe—Juvenile
literature. 3. Cave dwellers—Europe—Juvenile literature. 4. Europe—Antiquities—
Juvenile literature. [1. Prehistoric peoples. 2. Cave dwellers. 3. Glacial epoch.] I. Title.
GN772.2.A1 C66 2001
936—dc21   99-44202

CONTENTS

ACKNOWLEDGMENTS

If Alexander Marshack did not exist, neither would this book. He initiated my acquaintance with our Ice Age ancestors and the wonders of their art, and he has been unfailingly generous in providing information and making available some of his photographs and drawings for use here. I want to also give special thanks to Yvonne Vertut for her gracious help with obtaining photographs taken by her late husband, Jean Vertut.

Fellow staff members at the American Museum of Natural History, notably Eugene Bergmann and Ian Tattersall, have helped me through obstacles on the Ice Age landscape, and I particularly appreciate the efforts of the museum's library staff, present and past, in locating books and supplying pictures: Michelle Anastasia, Meghan Manahan, Barbara Mathe, Matthew Pavlick, Flora Rodriguez, and Annette Springer all deserve a vote of thanks.

Marcia Marshall, at Atheneum Books, was supportive on many counts; Jeffrey Saunders of the Illinois State Museum; John Shea of SUNY, Stony Brook; and Alexei Tikhonov of the Russian Academy of Sciences each gave welcome assistance. CNRS Publications, McGraw-Hill Companies, and Unesco Courier have generously allowed inclusion of material from their publications.

As for errors herein, I have no one to thank but myself.

PROLOGUE: THE CAVE

UP AN EASY hillside, down a flight of steps, and through a doorway into the blackness of the cave. The door shuts behind you and you stand there in the dark, waiting and wondering, not making a move. The silence encloses you. Then, suddenly, the lights are switched on.

Instantly, you know you are in a sacred place. Even though you came prepared for what you see, you can hardly believe your eyes. The black cave has become a radiant round chapel. Above your head a majestic gathering of animals encircles the pale, smooth walls and gently domed ceiling. Four huge bulls, painted in bold black and white, tower over the rest: a mingled procession of cows, fuzzy-headed horses, delicately antlered tiny deer—and a strange spotted animal, unlike any other, with two straight forward-pointing horns and a cowlike face. All seem to be bursting from within the walls they occupy. Their bodies bulge solidly with the bulging rock, and as you take a few steps forward, the thick neck of the bull stretches, or its eye looks at you a different way, because you see the bulges from a new angle, as you would in life.

Clearly, the animals rule this place; their spirit pervades it and their powerful presence inspires deep awe. You catch your breath and talk in whispers, if you talk at all.

In two galleries leading downward from the central chamber, the wonders of the cave continue. Golden galloping horses, charging bison, the heads and upper bodies of stags that seem to be swimming, a large jumping cow, and many others line the walls. And at the very end of one gallery, where the cave floor begins a sharp drop, is a scene of high drama: a horse is falling down a rock pillar, its legs sprawled helplessly in the air. Is the horse falling off a cliff, forced over the edge by pursuing hunters? We'll never know.

From the falling horse to the tiny deer and the largest bull, fifteen feet long, each animal is there in its essence, a masterpiece of freshness, fixed in a typical moment of action. Every turn of the head and movement of the leg, every detail from nose and ears to hooves and tail, is understood and presented in firm brush strokes. All are richly colored, sometimes with sprayed paint. The artists who created these grand friezes had all the skills they needed to express their feelings about the bulls and bison, mammoths and deer, and the other animals that dominated both the outer world they lived in and the inner world of the spirit.

Today we enter Lascaux by a bronze door, and we see its glorious images by electric light. But try to imagine it when the paintings were new. Imagine entering the cave through a hole in the ground and discovering its unknown chambers and galleries by the uncertain light of a torch. Imagine working there in the deep silence, cut off from the world outside, creating those huge bulls and galloping horses out of the contours in the rocks. Imagine gathering in this secluded place among the painted animals, perhaps singing or playing special music there or going through steps of a sacred dance amidst great flickering shadows. Imagine . . . imagine . . .

We will never penetrate the secrets of Lascaux. They will remain a mystery. But the late Ice Age has left many clues about the remarkable people who transformed the walls of Lascaux and many other caves, clues that we can follow to discover how they lived and to enter their world.

DISCOVERY: MAMMOTHS AND MEN

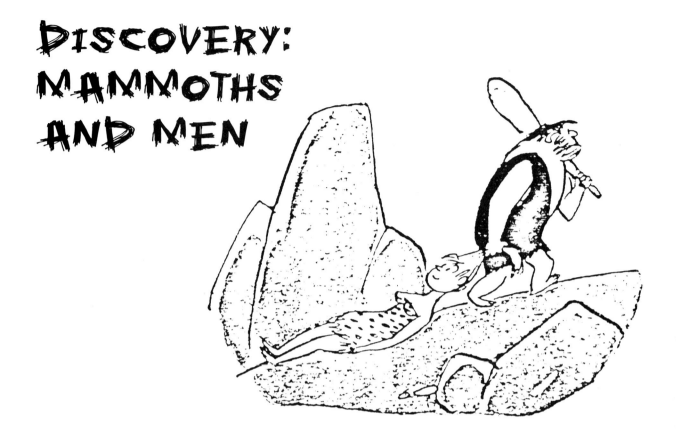

MEET THE ICE Age caveman, a fellow with long, tangled hair, a brutish face, and an animal skin draped over one shoulder. As he strides along barefoot, carrying a club, he often drags a helpless cavewoman by the hair. Lots of muscle, not much brain, and certainly no gentleman. He's a natural for cartoonists, but can you imagine him painting magnificent animal figures on a cave wall, like the ones in the cave of Lascaux?

A real man from the late Ice Age probably would have trouble with that idea, too. If he could whiz through time and land on your street, you might notice his trim Arctic-style clothing, but he would look much more like somebody you might see in the supermarket than the brute in the cartoons. So let's forget about the Ice Age caveman who keeps popping up in our cartoons.

Except that we can't forget him completely, because he's a holdover from a time not so long ago when nearly everybody thought he was the real thing and took him very seriously. Go back a little further in time and even the idea that any humans—cavemen or otherwise—could have existed during the Ice Age seemed ridiculous.

Like unknown territory, on Earth or beyond, the unknown past must be explored to be understood, and explorers who venture into the unknown usually have their problems with doubters. When Christopher Columbus started out on his daring voyage into the vast uncharted ocean, for example, few believed that he would ever be seen again, let alone find land on the other side of the ocean. However, to nearly everyone's surprise he returned, and doubters could be convinced that since he must have traveled a great distance during his long absence, he might have reached a new, faraway place.

People who reach into the unknown past have an even trickier set of problems than explorers like Columbus. Digging only a few yards into the ground may take you to objects thousands of years old. When your journey has covered such a short distance, it's naturally much harder to convince people that you've reached a faraway point in the past. Furthermore, there's nobody to explain what you've found, whether it's a spear point, an ancient ring, or a strange animal bone. The Earth's uncharted past has to be sorted out layer by layer, like a treasure hunt with very difficult clues.

As with the European discovery of the Americas, early discoveries in exploring the past came by accident. In Europe, a man plowing his fields or digging a hole for a well might come across a strangely chipped stone or an unfamiliar bone or tooth, obviously very old. That led people to dig deeper in places where such things had turned up, and they began to notice that the deeper layers they reached sometimes held bones and teeth that could belong to no land animal now known to exist. They were especially puzzled when they began finding human bones in the same layers as bones of vanished animals that could be identified as belonging to cave bears, woolly rhinoceroses, or mammoths.

The first find of that sort came in 1771, in a cave in the Jura Mountains of southwestern Germany. Caves are promising places to seek out the past because they have often been used by animals as dens and by humans for burials and other purposes. But even Johann Esper, the man who found the bones, could not believe that men and mammoths had lived at the same time. How could humans have existed as far back as the time when these long-extinct animals were walking around? The human bones must have found their way into the cave by accident.

While people continued to ponder this problem, they also continued searching caves for more clues to the past. Searching these caves took nerve. Some could be entered through a natural opening in the side of a hill, but

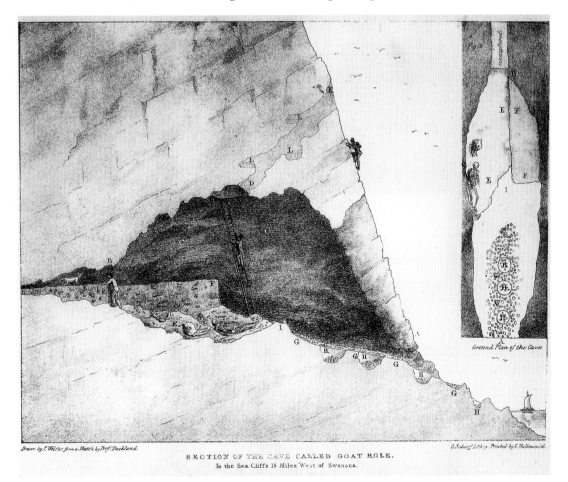

SECTION OF THE CAVE CALLED GOAT HOLE.
In the Sea Cliffs 15 Miles West of Swansea.

Seeking clues to the ancient past, nineteenth-century explorers sometimes risked descending into caves like this one in southern Wales. Sometimes they found remains of Ice Age humans.

to reach others, explorers had to clamber down a rope dangling through a hole on top. Once inside, they had to pick their way through narrow passages where they might get stuck or enter black galleries leading nowhere, their only light a torch that threw spooky, jumping shadows. Water often dripped on their heads and deep mud sometimes covered their feet as they probed, dug, and hacked, trying to unlock secrets of past human life. But when they found the puzzling bones and stones, the thrill of discovery was worth all the perils of the dark, damp journey.

And there were plenty of thrills for these explorers. Not only did they continue to find human bones and the bones of extinct animals together, but they saw that some of the animal bones showed signs of having been purposely cut with a tool, another clue that humans had been at work long before anyone had suspected. They also began to find human skulls. The caveman was starting to take shape.

Any human remains give clues about the person they once formed part of. A leg bone shows whether the person was tall or short, adult or child. The size and shape of a tooth may suggest the kind of food the person ate. And like the faces of living people, skulls from the past tell special stories about their owners in life. Even without a face, the slope of the forehead, the space for the brain, and the general shape present a picture that can make a long-gone person suddenly vivid.

Some of the first skulls found, unearthed near the Meuse River in Belgium from a cave called Engis, had no remaining face parts, but the skull was shaped very like yours and mine. Given that shape, it was possible to imagine a familiar face. These skulls lay with the bones of extinct rhinoceroses and mammoths and some chipped-stone tools. In the 1830s, sixty years after Johann Esper's find in Germany, most people were still not convinced that bones of men and mammoths could belong together. Much likelier, they thought, the human remains had been buried more recently and shifted into a lower underground layer as animals burrowed into the cave or a flood swept through it.

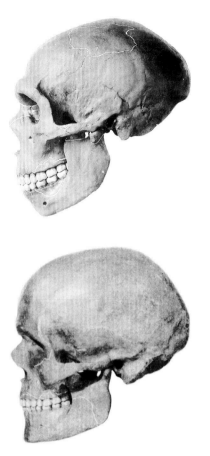

A Neanderthal skull (top) and one like ours (below) differ in shape. People in the 1850s decided that a newly discovered Neanderthal skull with a receding forehead, heavy brow, and very little chin must have belonged to some ancient brute.

Then came the find of a skull in Germany unlike any seen before. It came to light in 1856 in a quarry, once part of a cave, in the eastern valley of Neander—Neanderthal in German—which gave the skull its name. Like the skulls found in Belgium, this one lacked any remains of a face. What did remain, however, were a low forehead, large overhanging brow, and a rather flat top of the head. Something strange and definitely unfamiliar had been found.

A toothless jaw discovered in a Belgian cave not long afterward made the new puzzle even stranger. Little else had been found with the Neanderthal skull, but once again, mammoth bones and chipped stones appeared near the jaw. What's more, the jaw had no chin.

It's one thing to find ancestors who look as if they ought to be related to you, even if you can't account for their existence so long ago. It's quite another to find one who looks as if he didn't belong in polite society ever. Who wants an ancestor with a receding forehead, heavy brow, and no chin?

Scarcely anybody did, and many guesses were made to explain the skull and jaw, nearly all of them uncomplimentary. Some guessed that the skull had belonged to a man with a dread disease, although specialists who examined it thought otherwise. Maybe it belonged to an idiot or a wild man. In any case, people decided, a heavy brow and low forehead had to go with a flat, ugly face and a puny brain, and a jaw like that must have had fierce teeth for ripping prey. Clearly, such a skull and jaw must have survived from some sort of brute, as much ape as human, as vicious as he was stupid. The caveman had finally been recognized as real and found horrid in every respect.

More than a century later, we realize that the Neanderthals, who flourished from about 150,000 to 35,000 years ago, deserved a much better reception than they got. They might not win a modern beauty contest, but then again beauty is in the eye of the beholder. The truth is that they weathered a long stretch of the Ice Age very well. They had a brain as big as ours—in a few cases, even bigger; they had new ideas; they made tools that served their needs; and they got around. Neanderthal burials have been found in caves all the way from Central Asia to North Africa and many places in western Europe. Nevertheless, the memory of the fierce, mindless brute lingers on in our cartoons.

If the cartoon image fails to do justice to the Neanderthals, it is even further from the mark in picturing the Cro-Magnons who followed. These were the people whose skulls first appeared in the Belgian cave of Engis. They looked like us—or rather, we look like them. Now recognized as early modern humans, they were our remote direct ancestors. Explorers of the human past—more officially known as archeologists—have discovered that these remarkable people made beautifully decorated tools, complete suits of clothes, and a variety of ornaments. And they led rich, full lives that we know included creating music and the world's oldest surviving art masterpieces, such as those wonderful Lascaux wall paintings.

Long after Columbus landed on that first New World island in 1492, people still did not realize the extent of the continents he had found. Many frontiers had to be crossed, and the size of the newly found regions stretched again and again before the newcomers to the Americas had fully explored them. There were nearly impassable mountain ranges and treacherous rivers, hunger, fierce weather, and disease.

The much more recent discovery of Ice Age peoples and their world has also required the crossing of difficult frontiers, chiefly frontiers of understanding. In 1859, only a few years after the famous Neanderthal skull was found, the British naturalist Charles Darwin took the all-time daring plunge into the past when he first presented his theory of evolution to the world. He asked us to believe that our very existence is just an accident of nature, a late accident in a long series that piled up, one after the other, to develop all the Earth's plants and animals. He asked us to accept the idea that our ancestry goes back to human forms quite unlike ourselves—in fact, if we go back far enough, our ancestors were not human at all.

It still came as a shock, though, to admit that people who lived 25,000 or more years ago without metals, without farming, without cities, and without writing, could be our equals in thinking, perceiving, and imagining. In 1879, twenty years after Darwin put evolution on the map, disbelief greeted the first discovery of Ice Age paintings at the cave of Altamira in northern Spain, its ceiling decorated with a scene of amazingly lifelike bison. While people had begun to get used to the idea of the long course of the human past, they definitely were not ready to believe that accomplishments of the past could rival those of the present.

Great gaps still exist in our knowledge of the Ice Age and all that went before it; they always will. But as we continue to push our frontiers in exploring time, what we *have* learned about Ice Age people and their achievements gives us plenty of cause for wonder.

ROOMS WITH A VIEW

THE ICE AGE sounds cold, and it was: at its most intense times and places, it was a bleak world made of frozen ground, leaden skies, and fierce, shrill winds. In Antarctica, near the South Pole, such conditions still exist. If only Antarctic penguins could talk, they could give you an earful about what it's like to stand out in the open protecting a precious egg!

The present-day Antarctic ice sheet extends for many millions of square miles. If we were unlucky enough to have it arrive here, it would cover all of the continental United States. Huge as it is, however, this formidable stretch of ice takes second place to the ones that flourished about 20,000 years ago, during the late Ice Age. At that time the island of Manhattan lay under a sheet of ice 1,000 feet thick, about as high as the Empire State Building. At the same period in Europe, ice covered all of Scandinavia and reached well into Poland, Germany, and England. These ice sheets took so much water from the oceans that the outlines of continents looked different. Venice, now on the seashore, was 200 miles inland, and the British Isles were not islands at all but part of the European

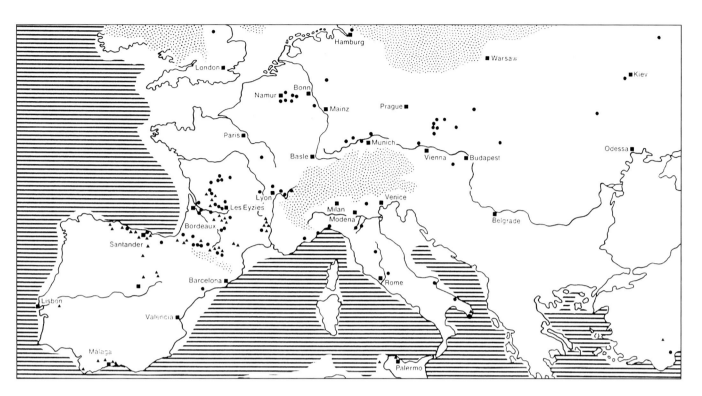

On this map, white areas outside present-day coastlines show where new land emerged around Europe's edges when immense glaciers sucked water from the seas 20,000 years ago. For example, land filled the space between England and the continent (upper left).

mainland. You could walk between the present sites of Paris and London.

Humans could not survive at all on the desolate, windswept land near the edge of that immense northern European ice sheet. There was nothing to eat and no place to hide. But a few hundred miles south of the looming ice, they could manage well enough. For example, in the region of south-western France now called the Dordogne, where the cave of Lascaux hides its secret images, winters were cold, snowy, and very windy—harsh but bearable. And during the much friendlier summers, temperatures reached into the fifties and the sun shone warmly.

The Dordogne is only one of many places in Europe where people lived during the late Ice Age, but it's a good place to look at because so many traces of life from that time have been found there. In this landscape of rolling hills and rivers that flow through wide, level valleys, caves go deep into some of the hillsides, and well above the valley floors the pale limestone cliffs bulge out where projecting rock hangs over large, flat ledges.

As people living close to nature, Ice Agers picking a place to settle certainly would have known what any experienced campers know: that the sunny, south side of a hill is warmer than the shady, north side, and thanks to the sun, it is drier too—and a sheltered place, out of the wind, makes the most desirable camping spot. A roomy cliffside ledge facing south, with its flat floor and an overhanging rock roof to provide protection from the worst weather, was well suited for a family or small group of families to set up camp. We know from remains like discarded animal bones and tools that small groups of Ice Agers in the Dordogne did indeed settle in these rock shelters.

The mouth of a south-facing cave offers similar advantages, but not its

Cliffs rising in the river valleys of southwestern France often have ledges with a rock overhang above, good places for Ice Agers to have camped.

interior. Deep inside some of the caves, Ice Age paintings and wall engravings remain—but not evidence of living there. Contrary to the caveman cartoon, a damp, dark, chilly cave is not an inviting place to hang your parka and call home.

The rock shelters that Ice Agers occupied were typically at least the size of a very large barn. Within this space they used separate areas for eating, sleeping, and doing work, such as making stone and bone tools. Not so different from our kitchens, bedrooms, and workshops or family rooms, minus the dividing walls, and there may have been some room dividers, too. Skins hung from an arrangement of branches would serve that purpose, for example. We can tell about the divided use of space by where remains have been found in some of the shelters: a trash pile of cast-off bones in one place, parts of stone or bone tools, waste flakes, and other debris that tool-making leaves behind in another, and traces of a hearth in a third spot.

The hearth, of course, tells us that fire was part of the picture—a very important part, too, in an Ice Age winter. Families living in a drafty rock shelter probably also made it more weatherproof by hanging animal skins on a framework of branches or by piling up brush across the open front of the shelter to shut out the attacking wind and the snow it drove in. They might also have used an early version of the sleeping bag at night: skins and possibly moss on the stone floor to lie on and more skins on top. The fur or hair on the skin would provide extra warmth.

We have to guess about this use of skins, which long ago decayed. We need not guess about fire, though. Fire leaves its traces in the form of the hearthstones that surrounded it and bits of leftover charred materials and ash. We know that fire had been in use for hundreds of thousands of years before our late Ice Agers came along, and we can also be quite sure that they knew how to start a fire by striking together the right kinds of stones to make hot sparks.

The benefits of fire, basic for survival in winter, also extended to the warmer months. Fire provided not only warmth but light after the sun went down, allowing Ice Agers (and many peoples before and after them) to eat, work, or sit companionably around the comforting hearth after dark. It also discouraged uninvited hungry animals from arriving while people slept and turning some member of the family into a midnight snack. For their own snacking, fire gave Ice Agers the option of cooking their food. Depending on who you are, cooked meat may or may not taste better to you than raw meat, but it is certainly easier to chew. Saving wear and tear on teeth meant that the teeth could last longer, which was all to the good in an era before dentists had arrived on the scene.

Protected in their rock shelter, our group of Ice Agers also had easy

Like a rock shelter, the mouth of a cave provides protection from snow and wind. Ice Agers camping in the mouth of Niaux, a cave in the Pyrenees Mountains, also had a grand view of the countryside.

access to the river water below and a sweeping view over the valley. Looking out, they could see the signs of tomorrow's storm or perhaps spot some animals moving about. With the river threading through grassy meadows, thickets, and scattered groves of trees in the valley below, their view presented a lovely scene during the year's greener period.

In contrast, the hilltop plateau beyond the valley, exposed to the weather at its worst, was mostly bare rock with mossy patches or tiny bushes and plants that hugged the ground for protection. For a brief time each year, during the late spring thaw, these miniature plants blossomed like a beautiful carpet with a burst of bright pink, yellow, and white flowers. In a very cold period, like the one 20,000 years ago, we can imagine how eagerly the Ice Agers welcomed that warm spring sun when it finally came again.

ANIMALS GALORE

THE PATCHWORK OF riverside marshes, flat meadows, thickets, bits of forest, and dry hilltop tundra that marked the Dordogne during the Ice Age had something for everyone. Each of these environments was home to the particular types of animals that could use the grasses, mosses, trees, or other special features it offered. Luckily for people who depended on hunting for much of their food, even in the coldest periods the view from the rock shelter was busy with animal life. The bones, antlers and horns, teeth and tusks found by archeologists in places where people lived, hunted, and piled up trash suggest that anything from a hare to a mammoth was fair game.

Think of an African game park where you see a herd of antelope grazing here, a hundred zebras galloping there, lions dozing under a spreading tree, elephants strolling through the long grass, and a rhinoceros or two charging along in the middle distance. Now change the climate and land—cold hills

Two birds carved by an Ice-Age artist on a piece of reindeer antler may possibly suggest a long-necked heron and, below it, a plump duck, summer visitors to the Dordogne's rivers.

and valleys instead of the warm flat plains of East Africa—and a different cast of characters appears. Looking over their Dordogne landscape, our Ice Agers would have seen shaggy horses instead of zebras galloping about, a group of bison grazing, and reindeer rather than antelope. The lions probably dozed in caves instead of under trees; the elephants were mammoths with long, curved tusks and high-domed head, and the rhinoceros charging in the middle distance was a woolly rhinoceros, well covered with two layers of hair to keep its bulky body warm. Then there were the smaller animals usually hidden from sight, such as weasels, hares, badgers, and mouse-like voles and other rodents.

In the summer there were the birds: flocks of ducks, swans, and geese on the river; long-legged herons, plover, and other waders in marshy places; colorful songbirds; and many others. Overhead floated larger hawks ready to swoop for the next meal. At the right time of year, the rivers thronged with crowds of salmon, pike, and other fish, and from time to time even some seals. And let's not forget insects. We know, for example, that grasshoppers appeared at some times and places, because an artist engraved a tiny image on a bone of one about to be snapped up by a bird.

It seems remarkable that such a crush of diverse animals, many of them large, could have managed to survive in that one little chilly section of France no bigger than the state of Massachusetts. Very remarkable when you consider how much grazing room is needed by a large plant-eating animal: one bison bull can chew his way through a whole acre of short grass such as the Dordogne might have had in a few weeks. We have to conclude that in the Ice Age world the Dordogne was an unusually favored area.

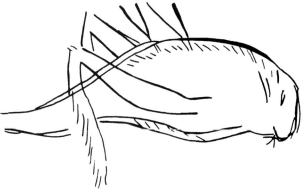

Ice Agers took note of the animals in their landscapes, from mammoths to insects. The tip of a bird's beak appears above the grasshopper's back.

With the snowbound Pyrenees Mountains to the south and forbidding glaciers to the north and east, the little river valleys and their flanking cliffs offered both people and animals the best conditions in the region.

Which animals thrived best depended on whether the ice was pushing close enough to make the severest winters or retiring to a distance that allowed an easier climate. We know from observing animals today that the musk ox, well bundled in its long hair, doesn't mind braving a winter hilltop where the freezing wind will blow away snow and expose the dried grass underneath. The ibex, a large goatlike animal with heavy horns, is at home on cold, steep hillsides—the colder and steeper, the better. The bison will face out a blizzard, protected by the thick wool on its head and shoulders. Though the mammoth is gone, remains found in places from western Europe to Siberia show that it, too, could brave the wide-open winter spaces, snugly enclosed in a woolly undercoat and a layer of coarse outer hairs. The reindeer is still another cold-weather customer.

But the frosty weather that suits the reindeer does not suit the European red deer, which resembles our elk, or the smaller roe deer, nearly so well. Bones found at places in the Dordogne dating from different periods of the Ice Age tell us that these woodland deer became more common and reindeer less so as the climate slowly warmed over the centuries. In this warming period 15,000 to 10,000 years ago that brought the Ice Age to an end, the view from the rock shelter would have been woodsier. The forests that grew up teemed with deer and other wildlife, including the aurochs, a larger and of course untamed ancestor of modern cattle. There were big brown bears and lynxes and wolves, not to mention the woodland contingent of foxes, squirrels, beavers, and mice.

While the red deer continues to inhabit modern European forests, its strange relative, the giant elk, vanished with the Ice Age itself. With antlers that spread ten or more feet across—twice the spread of moose antlers—this extra-large deer must have been a sight to behold as it moved across the countryside. Examples of its immense antlers and also of its bones have been found, but its habits remain a mystery. We don't know for sure whether this unusual animal lived in the forest or out in the open, or why it died out. Maybe its huge antlers turned out to be too much of a good thing and it couldn't manage them.

The giant elk is one of a number of Ice Age species now gone forever. Among others, they include the cave bear, the woolly rhinoceros, and, of course, the mammoth. Luckily for us, the Ice Age artists made remarkably vivid portraits of these vanished animals, so that we have a good idea what they looked like in life. We also have bones and teeth, unearthed by diggers into the past, to show us their sizes and shapes. And from time to time other surprising clues turn up.

For example, quite a number of frozen mammoths have been found over a long stretch of land on the north coast of Siberia. How they came to be there is not altogether clear. One idea suggests that during the long warming spell that ended the Ice Age, mammoths inhabiting the Siberian

In colder times and places, especially the grasslands of eastern Europe and Siberia, mammoths were very much part of the landscape. These drawings represent a few of the many mammoth images that Ice Agers engraved in bone or antler.

grasslands migrated north every year in search of cooler, more comfortable summer temperatures. The many that died there sank down into mud and frozen ground through the seasons of thawing and freezing, to be preserved until modern times. Some are so well preserved that we know the mammoth's summer coat was red, the color of a red fox. So many mammoth skeletons have also surfaced in that area through the years that certain places rank as mammoth graveyards.

For every frozen mammoth body or skeleton that has come to light in this unexpected way, there had to be many more mammoths on the scene whose remains disappeared forever. Imagine watching a herd of red mammoths lumbering across the grassy landscape! Though fewer mammoths lived in the Dordogne than in Siberia, we can see them in the Ice Agers' lifelike engravings and paintings of this awesome red beast, its little eye almost glinting and its long, curving tusks ready to take on all comers.

Mammoths have long been extinct, but every now and then, when summer thaws melt ice in the far north, a well-preserved frozen mammoth comes to light. This baby mammoth, discovered in 1988, died 30,000 years ago in northwestern Siberia.

KEEPING WARM

PUT YOURSELF IN the shoes of an Ice Ager looking out from a rock shelter at the winter world, when conditions might please a mammoth, and you quickly understand why shoes, hats, and other warm clothes stood high on the list of necessities—another blow to the cartoon caveman in his bare feet and knee-length animal skin. The cartoon is right about one thing, however: Ice Agers did make their snug outfits from animal skins.

Like other materials used for clothing, animal skins don't last once they have been discarded or buried with the person wearing them. They soon fall apart and decay. But we have other clues to tell us that Ice Agers wore well-fitting, warm clothes: not only boots or moccasins but hats or hoods, pullover shirts, trousers, and outer cloaks. The whole outfit must have looked quite a lot like what more recent Eskimos and Siberian peoples have traditionally worn in the far north.

Like Ice Agers of the ancient past, some of the peoples living in northeastern Siberia a century ago decorated their animal-skin clothing with beads.

Rows of hundreds of bone beads once decorated the clothing of a woman buried 25,000 years ago in Russia. The way they lay along her bones provided a clue that she had worn a shirt and trousers similar to more recent Eskimo apparel.

While animal skins don't last once they are buried, teeth, bones, and mammoth tusks have long staying power in the ground. If you're lucky enough to find these hard materials made into beads and other ornaments, you may be onto something very interesting.

That was the case at Sungir, not far from modern Moscow, where Russian archeologists discovered remains of an Ice Age settlement about 25,000 years old. Investigating the grave of a woman buried there, they found that at least 3,500 little beads and some other ornaments still lay more or less in rows scattered over the bones.

Given an extraordinary clue like this one, the right detectives can decipher things about the past that we never could have guessed. For example, from the way three rows of bone beads and one of silver fox teeth lay around the skull, the archeologists recognized that these ornaments once decorated the edge of the woman's cap or hood. Other rows of beads traced the outlines of her shirt, trousers, shoes, and cloak. In addition, 25 bracelets of mammoth tusk ivory, and some bead bracelets as well, remained on the bones of each arm.

Clearly, this was a burial fit for a grand personage. Try figuring out how many hours of work would be needed to cut out 3,500 little beads, drill a

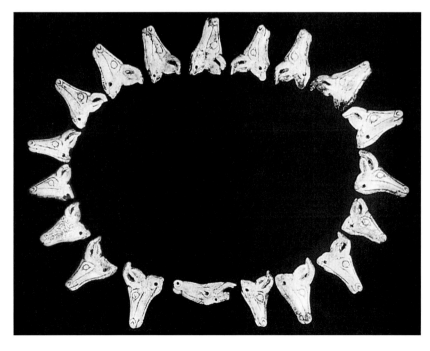

These ivory ibex heads—and one horse head (bottom)—once formed an unusually elegant necklace, perhaps strung together with a strand of sinew. It probably belonged to an important person.

hole through each, and attach them in neat rows to the edges of a suit of clothes. You can easily see that unless there are lots of people with time for such a project, not everybody could dress in such elegant style—elegance that even a modern person of high standing might be hard put to match. So this remarkable clue of beads also tells us that some people in the group at Sungir rated special treatment. The taste for costly finery as a way to show personal importance apparently hasn't changed much in 25,000 years.

As with the thousands of little beads found in the Sungir burials, making the animal skin clothes they once decorated took a lot of time, skill, and the right tools. Neatly skinning a large animal such as a reindeer is no easy job; but judging from the skill of modern Eskimos and others, the Ice Age hunter no doubt wielded his stone knife with a sure hand and made short, tidy work of skinning his catch. Again taking our model from Eskimos and other northern hunting groups, we can guess that once the hunter had provided the skin, chances are that women of the group, including young girls, busied themselves preparing it. Chances are too, that this work kept them busy indeed, especially as winter approached.

Many stone scrapers remain from the Ice Age. A woman could hold one of these smallish pieces of stone in her hand and use the roughly flattened end or the side edge, depending on which type of scraper she chose, to scrape off the fat and other tissue from the inside of the skin. Typically, the skin may then have been stretched tight over stakes or weighted around the edges with stones so that it would dry free of wrinkles. As it dried, it also stiffened, however.

Ice Ager women probably solved this problem as many Eskimo women have done—with their teeth. If you chew on a skin for long enough, inch by inch, it softens and becomes flexible. At least one Ice Age skull has been found with teeth worn down in a way that suggests much skin chewing. Most of this chewing probably went on in the fall, when reindeer skins are at their best. In early fall, the bucks eat heartily to prepare for the mating season, when they will spend their time banging each other's antlers and skip dinner.

Having chewed the skin to a workable softness, the women (we suppose) could begin cutting it into pieces of the right shapes and sizes to make cozy winter outfits for one and all. Like skinning an animal, this project called for a good eye and a steady hand—mistakes could result in ill-fitting clothes or wasting valuable material that had taken much time and labor to prepare. Then came the job of putting the pieces together. The Ice Age woman solved *this* problem with one of the great Ice Age inventions, the needle.

Small as they are, plenty of smoothly tapered, polished needles, each with a neatly drilled eye, have been found in Ice Age settlements. We refer to them as bone needles, but they were commonly made from splinters of reindeer antler, a somewhat harder material. Inventing a needle with an eye that could hold and carry the sewing thread was a master stroke for people who needed to make clothes that would keep them warm and dry, and the needle hasn't changed in design since an Ice Age supergenius dreamed it up about 20,000 years ago.

A sewing needle is a small household item, but try making clothes or mending them without it! Now we use steel instead of slivers of reindeer antler, but the design has hardly changed since Ice Agers invented the needle with an eye 20,000 years ago.

This little piece of equipment, which has been in continuous use longer than any other we know of, made a big difference, because it allowed stitchers to sew a fine seam in a way that was impossible before. Until they had the needle, people had to use a sharp-pointed tool to punch each hole in the skin pieces and then separately lace the pieces together. Doing the job that way meant bigger holes, clumsier seams, and more chance that icy air or water could come through. It also meant slower work. What's the hurry? you may ask. Well, if you needed to make a warm, waterproof suit of clothes for each member of the family, you might be glad to save all the time you could. The needle also made possible finicky work such as sewing all those little beads to the edges of trousers and hats.

No thread remains from Ice Age times, but we can turn again to the Eskimos for a clue. They divide the sinews from a caribou's back into very fine, strong filaments, excellent for use as sewing thread. If the sinew gets wet after the clothes are finished, so much the better. It will swell slightly to fill the sewing holes even tighter than before.

Dressed in their well-tailored, warm suits, complete with hood and boots to match, our Ice Agers living in the Dordogne could survey the winter world from their rock shelters and get on with their business, outdoors or at home.

As shown in this drawing, the markings on the figure suggest fur.

HUNTING BIG GAME

FOR ICE AGERS, like the rest of us, getting enough to eat had to be high on the list of important business. That meant having meat on hand, especially in winter, when food plants disappear. Luckily for the people living in their Dordogne rock shelters, hunters usually didn't have to look far to see several reindeer bobbing their heads as they meandered along seeking out patches of "reindeer moss"—a form of lichen—or maybe a group of horses or bison or even a huge aurochs.

Counting the number of bones remaining from different kinds of animals in places where Ice Agers lived tells us which ones the hunters favored. Reindeer usually come out way ahead. While an aurochs weighing a ton could provide a lot more meat than a 200-pound reindeer, hunting an aurochs would have been a very risky project. If an angry bull decided to charge, chances are that at least one of the hunters pursuing it would never have hunted again. Hunting accidents probably happened all too often.

Reindeer were a lot easier to catch, and they also were very plentiful in this part of Ice Age Europe. The Native Americans, or American Indians, who dominated the Great Plains, are said to have used every part of the buffalo but the bellow. Reindeer don't bellow, they grunt, but Ice Agers found the reindeer equally useful. If they caught enough reindeer, their families would be quite well supplied not only with dinner but also with materials for most of what they needed.

But if you imagine reindeer moving along in great herds like Plains buffalo, you're on the wrong reindeer track. Great herds are possible in relatively flat, open expanses like the tundra or grasslands of Alaska, where thousands of caribou—the North American version of reindeer—migrate long distances in spring and fall seeking the best places to feed. In the Ice Age river valleys of France, where reindeer shared a hilly landscape with so many other animals, they banded in small groups and didn't travel as far from season to season.

In places where people hunt, experience teaches reindeer and other game animals that the presence of a human is likely to mean bad news. To survive, they must be alert to possible life-threatening signals and respond fast. Thanks to their keen senses of smell and hearing, they quickly discover such dangers. When alarmed, they also can flee much faster than a hunter can pursue them.

The hunter can't hear, sniff, or run nearly as well as the reindeer, but he tries to tip the balance by understanding the habits of the animals he hunts and what they are likely to do next. Such awareness is at least as important to a hunter's success as the weapon he carries. Looking at an Ice Age artist's image of the sleek, streamlined body of a lion moving forward or the sturdy posture of a bison, head down and hump up, we can see beyond a doubt how well Ice Agers observed and understood the animals in their world. Clearly, these ancient hunters knew that keeping well hidden is often the key to success. If you want to catch reindeer or other large animals, you can't let them discover that you're there until you're ready to spring.

From whiskers and alert ears to upright tail, this beautifully detailed engraving of a running lion shows how carefully Ice Agers observed the behavior of animals—the first requirement for successful hunting. Wisely, they did not hunt lions.

Hunters also knew that, among other habits, reindeer tend to follow the same paths repeatedly. Observing this pattern, the hunters could have used any of several methods favored by more recent reindeer hunters in the Arctic region. For example, a line of snares can be set up along a narrow stretch of a reindeer trail—perhaps long strips of rawhide tied into large loops and attached to low branches of a bush or small tree. As the reindeer come along, one or two hidden hunters suddenly make a big noise so that the reindeer break into a run. Fleeing in alarm, one or more of the animals might get entangled in a snare, and other hunters lying in wait can move in with their spears.

Another method is to dig pitfalls, hiding the pits with small branches and dried grass. As with snares, if a reindeer falls into a pit along the trail, concealed hunters can quickly go into action. Hunters everywhere know that riverbanks where animals regularly go to drink are good places to set up an ambush, and the hunters can also hide at places like river crossings and attack as a group of reindeer begins to wade in.

Reindeer can be fooled, too. A hunter can crouch low and disguise him-self, using a cape of reindeer skin and holding up branched sticks for "antlers." To avoid having the reindeer identify him by scent, he stays downwind—that is, so that the wind blows from the reindeer toward the hunter. Though wary of humans, reindeer are curious; one may actually move closer to investigate this other "reindeer" and come within range of a spear. Eskimo caribou hunters have stalked animals this way, and Plains Indians, equipped with bows and arrows, used to disguise themselves and stalk buffalo in similar fashion.

Ice Agers may or may not have had bows and arrows—it's one of the questions that specialists have argued about—but they certainly had plenty of spears. Spear points made of stone, bone, or reindeer antler have been

The nineteenth-century artist George Catlin observed how Plains Indian buffalo hunters wore a wolfskin disguise to avoid detection as they approached the buffalo. Ice Agers may have done something similar, using a reindeer-skin cape and antlers to lure reindeer within spearing distance.

found in a great range of places. And spears became much more powerful when used with an amazing Ice Age invention: the spear-thrower.

Most of us would never guess by looking at a spear-thrower that it could have such a powerful effect on a spear. It's a piece of reindeer antler, about a foot long, shaped into a shaft with one end curved into a solid hook. The other, straight end serves as a handle. The hunter lays this little shaft along the underside of his much longer spear and wedges the back end of the spear into the spear-thrower's hook.

Now for the tricky part. Holding the spear and the handle end of the spear-thrower together, the hunter raises his arm and hurls the spear. As he thrusts his arm forward, releasing the spear, he keeps hold of the spear-thrower's handle. The hook end pivots forward to a position straight behind the departing spear. This action gives the spear an extra shove so that it can travel more than twice as far with much greater force. This advantage allows the hunter to throw his spear more effectively from a safer distance—good luck for him, especially if he's pursuing a large, dangerous animal.

To understand how the spear-thrower works, try this bit of action: With your hand facing forward at shoulder height, hold a long pencil at the eraser end so that the other end points toward your shoulder. Move your arm as if you're throwing a ball and you'll see that the pencil will then point straight ahead, like an extension of your outstretched arm. In effect, the spear-thrower does its job of giving the

Inventing the spear-thrower greatly improved Ice Agers' chances of success in hunting. They decorated some with carved animals, such as this long-necked horse.

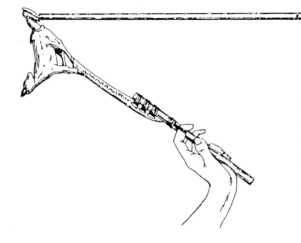

The spear-thrower is basically a rod, hooked at one end to hold the back of the spear. When the hunter hurls the spear, the spear-thrower he still holds rapidly pivots forward, from beneath the spear to behind it, giving the spear much extra force.

spear more distance and speed by extending both the length and leverage of a hunter's arm. That's a complicated idea, and inventing this little device took some very fancy thinking.

Small wonder that the spear-thrower continued in use for thousands of years in many parts of the world. That includes the Americas, where it is commonly known by its Aztec name, the atlatl.

A hunter with a good strong arm and a spear-thrower could send a spear whizzing through the air for well over 100 feet. Lying in wait at the right place or stalking his target animal, he might bring down a reindeer as it moved along through the snow. If he could sneak up on a small herd of horses or bison busy grazing, he might have luck with one of those animals, too. But Ice Age hunters would often have decided, as more recent hunters have done, that it was more effective to get together and drive a group of bison or horses to their doom than to go it alone pursuing single animals. That approach also works for hunting reindeer.

Like sheep, bison and horses tend to cluster together and amble along in a band or herd, making it easier for hunters to drive them in a desired direction. If they are frightened, the amble changes to a run, but where the leader goes, the rest follow.

Even in recent times, people in some parts of the world have continued to use the spear-thrower for hunting and sometimes for war. In this photo from about 1950, Australian Aborigines conduct a peace ceremony, using spear-throwers to hurl spears with the points removed.

By quietly approaching a small herd from behind and suddenly making loud noises and wild gestures, hunters can alarm a group of bison or horses and cause them to rush forward. Others posted at spots along the way force the fleeing herd toward the hunters' goal. Drive the animals into deep snow in winter or a wet sticky bog in spring, and they'll slow down or get stuck. Or drive them along a dead-end path into a corral, and they'll be trapped. When some of the animals get stuck, the hunters can move closer and hurl their spears. This technique has long been known to reindeer hunters in the far north, who build a stone corral at a strategic place to catch the animals.

Besides driving animals to a place where they are trapped, hunters can drive them over the edge of a cliff. The dramatic scene in the cave of Lascaux that shows a horse plunging down a steep rock face, its legs askew, may or may not picture an actual event, but such an event was certainly possible. Solid evidence pointing to this hunting method comes from southern Russia, among other places, where bones from many hundreds of bison skeletons have been found at the foot of a cliff below a spot where a group of Ice Agers had camped. The skeletons may have piled up over time, as the Ice Agers repeatedly returned to this place for part of the year and hunted the bison in the area.

The "drive" approach could be used for hunting even a large, fierce animal like an aurochs or a mammoth. If you hope to get the best of an angry bull, one form of insurance is to get it stuck in the mud or in a corral, where it can't charge at you. That goes for an angry mammoth, too.

Ice Age mammoths were grass eaters, unlike today's elephants, which chomp on leaves and brush. There weren't very many of them in the rock shelter areas of France and northern Spain, but herds of these impressive beasts moved about on the huge grassy plain, with its rivers and rolling hills, that sweeps across much of central Europe and far into Asia. People living in parts of this immense region depended on the mammoth for many of their needs, using the bones and ivory tusks to make everything from tools to beads. In areas with few trees to provide wood, fresh mammoth bones, which contained fat, also could be burned as fuel for cooking and heating. What the reindeer did for Ice Agers living in southwestern France, the mammoth did for people farther east.

Undoubtedly, Ice Agers hunted mammoths. Many mammoth bones have been found at places where they camped. But while the bones prove that Ice Agers made use of lots of mammoth parts, not much is known about how they hunted mammoths or how well they succeeded. Like lions chasing a herd of antelope, human hunters know that a good strategy is to go after a young or weak member of the group, and it's true that at some places the bones that remain are mostly from young mammoths. Lacking a lion's strength and sprinting power, Ice Agers may have used various techniques, possibly including grassland fires, to drive mammoths into a bog, or perhaps they made pitfalls, concealed with branches and long grasses, along mammoth routes to riverbanks. Near two places in Spain where Ice Agers camped, bones from mammoths that died in swamps have been found. A bigger surprise comes from Lehringen, in western Germany, where remains of a mammoth stuck with a wooden spear date to 120,000 years ago—way back in Neanderthal times.

People who have looked into the subject think that there were tons of bones and tusks lying about from mammoths that had died of natural causes, a much readier source of material than hunting down a mammoth. As for the meat, if hunters could kill one mammoth or find one that had just died, their group would be supplied for a long time. The Ice Age certainly had its discomforts, but it also had some benefits, such as a natural deep freeze for preserving meat.

MARKING TIME

ANIMALS SUCH AS bison and reindeer typically migrate as the seasons change to find the best feeding grounds. Each year, they also assemble in large groups; that is the time when mating happens. Then they break into smaller bands, and the males often separate from the females and young. Whatever their pattern of comings and goings, they repeat it from one year to the next.

As people for whom animal watching must have been an everyday, lifetime business, Ice Agers certainly knew these patterns, and their art often shows what animals were up to at different times of the year. For example, a cow and a calf engraved on opposite sides of a bone disk reflect spring, the time when new calves are born, while a stag painted with its mouth open as if baying at a rival brings to mind fall, the time when stags do battle to win a favored female. Seasonal images such as these include a long list of animals that came and went during the year—even a male and female seal swimming along a piece of reindeer antler in a summer scene that also includes salmon.

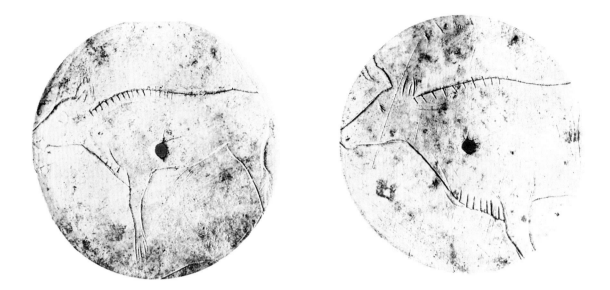

Like many other Ice Age images, the cow and calf engraved on the two sides of a bone disk suggest a seasonal idea: in this case spring, when the young of many animals are born.

The proof of how Ice Agers keyed their lives to the seasons lies in the many remains of campsites all across Europe, including the one in southern Russia where the bison skeletons lay. These are places where they set up housekeeping for seasonal hunting. In southern France, rock shelters provided well-protected headquarters for winter hunting, when many kinds of animals took shelter in the valleys. But when the weather eased up, many of the animals moved to different areas and so did the people who hunted them.

Animals take off when a change in temperature or light or some other sign of seasonal change sets the time for moving. Sometimes they go singly, sometimes in small groups or in large herds. They find food as they move along and keep warm in their well-padded, furry skins.

For people, it's another story. Unlike the reindeer whose paths they slowly followed, families of Ice Agers needed to equip themselves for the journey with food to eat, tools for catching or collecting more food on the way, the means to make a fire, and possibly extra shoes. We don't know how these things and other necessary items might have been carried—did Ice Agers have reindeer-hide backpacks? Maybe. Babies could have been carried in a type of backpack too, or in front, held in a shoulder sling.

Obviously, Ice Agers couldn't go to the store at the last minute and pick up the spear points they might need in their travels or a skin bag for collecting food plants. They had to have time to make or prepare whatever they wanted to take along, from spears to dried meat. To be ready to pack up and go at short notice, they needed to know well in advance when the animals might leave.

The question is: How do you keep one jump ahead of the reindeer, knowing before the time comes when they're going to migrate? A possible answer: Don't depend only on nearby signals like melting snow, because they may come too late. Look at the night sky and keep track of its patterns, especially the moon's comings and goings.

It doesn't take an astronomer with a high-powered telescope to see how the moon changes, growing from no moon at all to full moon and shrinking back again to begin a new cycle. American Indians have long watched the moon go through its paces. They have names for its cycles that relate to their lives. For example, the Haida of the north Pacific coast call the December moon cycle "Food Almost Gone Moon," and the Penobscot, across the continent in Maine, call the April cycle "Swimming Trout Moon." For centuries, many Indian sky watchers have recorded the moon's behavior by marking dots, lines, crescents, or other symbols on sticks or rocks.

Calendars help people foresee and plan for seasonal changes. Some American Indian tribes marked the moon's monthly cycles, night by night, on a long stick, like the one held by the Winnebago chief in this nineteenth-century painting.

Jean Vertut

Like many animals painted by Ice Age artists in the cave of
Lascaux, this bull seems almost ready to jump off the walls.

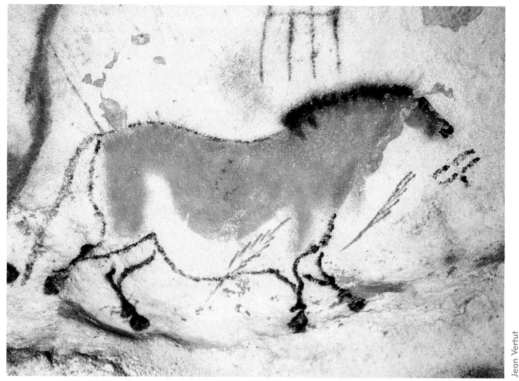

A few strong lines, a fuzzy mane, and chunky hooves capture the essence and motion of the small, short-legged horses that roamed Ice Age landscapes. This superb painting in the cave of Lascaux is often called the "Chinese horse" because it reminds people of Chinese ink-paintings.

Ice Age hunters sometimes drove animals over a cliff. The painted horse falling down a steep wall in the cave of Lascaux perhaps suggests that idea.

Carved animals sometimes decorated spear-throwers, an important Ice Age invention that helped make hunting more successful. Here two headless ibexes, locked together, form part of a spear-thrower made from a piece of antler.

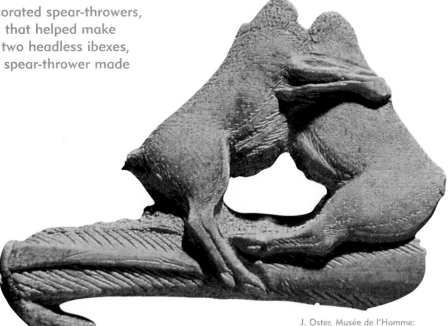

The ibex, a large goat suited to life in steep, cold mountains, is among the animals painted on walls deep in the Pyrenees Mountains cave of Niaux.

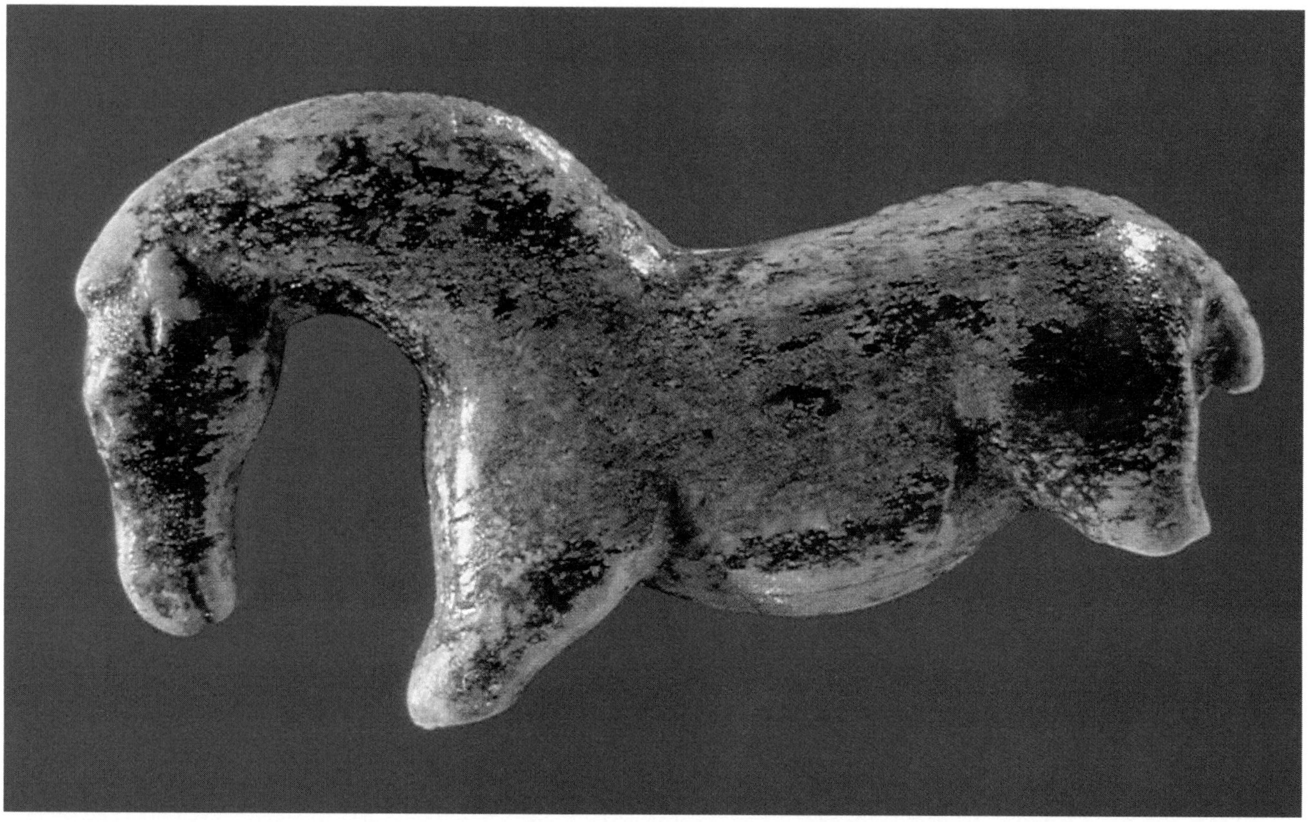

Alexander Marshack

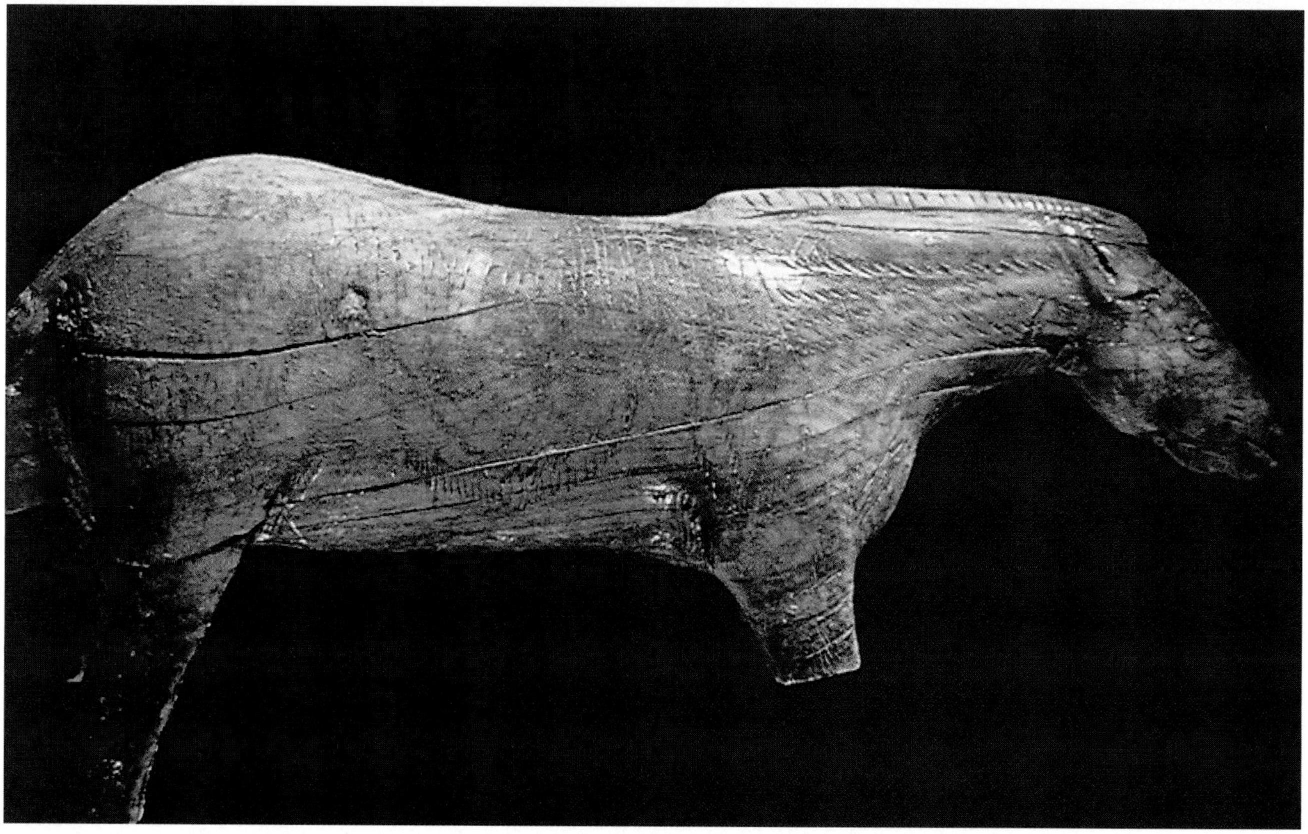

Musée des Antiquités Nationales; American Museum of Natural History

Compared with the much earlier horse above, this ivory horse carved about 14,000 years ago has more realistic details, but is it horsier? You decide.

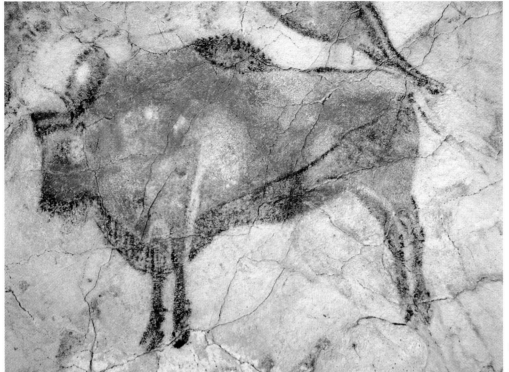

A large scene of many bison, standing like this one or lying down, covers the ceiling of the cave of Altamira, in northern Spain, the first cave with extensive animal paintings ever discovered.

Amazingly, two bison sculptured in clay some 15,000 years ago have survived deep in the cave of Tuc d'Audoubert, in the Pyrenees region of southern France. The difference between the heavily built male and the smaller female above him can be clearly seen.

From the well-made hole to the notched border and the engraved design, the workmanship on this little pendant shows how skillfully Ice Agers used their stone tools. The actual pendant, found at a rock shelter in France, is two inches long.

Though arranged here as a necklace, these large animal teeth and smaller pieces of bone and stone from an Ice Age rock shelter were probably made to be used separately as pendants or as beads attached to clothing. Many examples of ornaments have been found at places where Ice Agers lived.

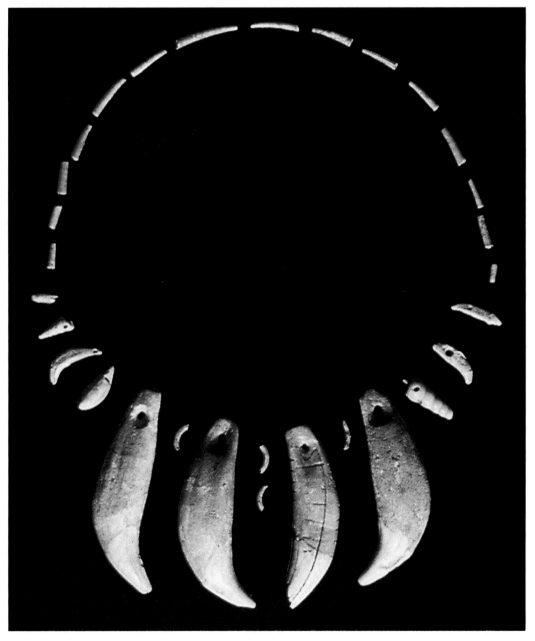

Top: This long-necked carved bird, found in a French rock shelter, could be a goose or a swan. Water birds like these visited the rivers in southwestern France during Ice Age summers, especially in the warming period before the Ice Age ended.

Middle: The scene carved on a piece of reindeer antler by an Ice Age artist about 10,000 years ago shows several hunters pursuing a large aurochs. Some people think that the first hunter holds a bow, possibly an Ice Age invention.

Bottom: Neckbands, a bracelet, and an anklet adorn the two naked figures engraved on a piece of bone from a French Pyrenees rock shelter, and the figure in front is marked with a barb sign and darts. Perhaps a story well-known to Ice Agers explained the meaning of this unusual image.

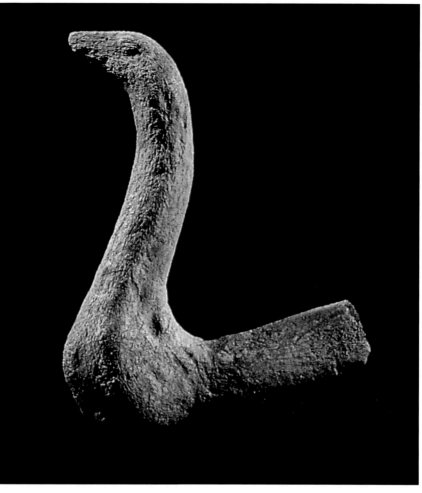

This painting on a wall in the cave of Lascaux suggests deer swimming across a river. Ice Agers must have often seen such a sight at the time when deer migrate from one area to another.

The giant elk, with immense antlers spanning ten feet, inhabited some areas of Ice Age Europe but disappeared forever as the climate warmed. In this Charles Knight painting, based on giant elk remains, those huge antlers look like quite a burden to carry around.

A stick marked with the moon's nightly appearance can measure time the way a marked ruler or tape measures space. Because moon cycles, like animal migration and many other patterns in nature, repeat from one year to the next, once you have the markings set down, you can use them again later. The stick that you marked last year can be consulted this year for clues about seasonal events to come.

As with measuring the length of a room or the distance between two trees, the important thing to know is where your time measurement begins and ends. The starting point might be the full moon that follows the days when trees and bushes begin losing their leaves as fall arrives, for example. Then you can count the marks on the stick that show how many days or moon cycles will pass until food-almost-gone time, and you can prepare for that skimpy period. Or you can use the full moon following the first breakup of ice on the river in late winter, and count how many moon cycles or parts of a cycle you have for making or repairing the nets and fish traps you will need to be ready when trout-swimming time comes. Whether the markings record one moon cycle, several, or more, your marked stick or rock is the calendar providing you with the advance news.

The enlarged detail of a Winnebago calendar stick shows how it was marked every day to record the moon's changing appearance. The two horizontal lines indicate the moonless nights between old and new moons.

Amazing as it seems, a number of small stones and bones have been found marked in a way suggesting that Ice Agers may have been up to the same sort of thing that American Indians were doing thousands of years later. Intrigued by the tiny markings and their possible meaning, Alexander Marshack, who has long studied Ice Age art, began examining some of these stones and bones with a microscope some years ago. At first, he could hardly believe his own eyes when he counted how the markings often fell into groups that seemed to follow moon cycles. Other people were even more doubtful that such a system could have been possible thousands of years before writing or arithmetic existed.

The first calendars? Quite possibly. Series of marks made by Ice Agers on different bones seem to match the moon's nightly changes through one or more cycles.

By now, enough examples have been discovered and studied to make the idea of Ice Age moon calendars quite convincing. Not only are the markings grouped as if to show different moon cycles, but in some cases they include crescents and full circles like the phases of the moon itself. As with the Indians, Ice Agers possibly could have made use of such a system to prepare for the seasons to come. And as with peoples the world over, ancient and modern, their calendars also could have served as a guide for holding events to celebrate, to ask spirits for help, or to thank them for providing it.

ALL SORTS OF SHELTERS

ICE AGERS LIVING in southwestern France and northern Spain took advantage of the rock shelters in their landscapes, especially in winter—a lot easier than building a home from scratch to keep out icy blasts of wind and swirling snow. But when they followed the animals seeking greener grass, they had to leave these ready-made homes and devise some other type of shelter. The tents made of hide held up by branches that these campers might have set up under the open sky are long gone, but groups of these ancient tents or huts have left some evidence showing that they once stood there.

For example, to set a branch upright as a tent post, a hole has to be dug to sink one end of the branch in the ground—the same idea as setting up posts for a fence. The branch will decay as time passes, but the hole where it stood sometimes remains. Such holes have been discovered at a place near Nice, in southern France, where people built a shelter 350,000 years ago, long before the time of our Ice Agers. Given the right conditions, an impression made in the ground can settle in and last a long while.

Holes in the ground by themselves would be hard to connect with ancient humans at work. When they turn up with other remains such as stone tools or stones arranged to form a hearth, the connection becomes clearer. And if the hearth contains bits of ash from wood or other fuel once burned there, special kinds of tests can often determine how long ago people camped at that spot. Anything that was once alive, like wood or bone, can be tested this way to discover its age. Stone can't be dated, but styles of shaping stone tools changed over thousands of years, providing another guide to when an ancient campsite might have been used. And stones, or sometimes antlers, forming a ring or other shape around the edge of a site, could have been used to hold a tent's hide covering firmly in place. The bones of animals give a different kind of clue. If some of them come from young animals, for example, the animals were probably hunted in summer, soon after the time of year when horses, deer, and others give birth.

The many Ice Agers who lived in regions where no rock shelters exist had to build all their shelters, summer and winter. While a summer tent could be a simple structure of poles and hide, maybe something like a Plains Indian tipi, a winter hut had to be sturdier, with thicker walls to keep in whatever warmth a fire supplied. One guess is that walls were made of stones or branches with clods of earth to hold them in place and fill in all the gaps. The walls could have been anchored in a foundation of stones placed around the edges of the hut floor. In fact, the whole floor could have been covered in stone for insulation from the frozen ground underneath. At some sites, that's the way things look.

You can build from the ground up, and also from the ground down. Animals such as rabbits and chipmunks dig burrows for protection from winter cold. People sometimes burrow into the ground too: Eskimos in

Scattered oblong pits at an eastern European site may have been the floors of tentlike dwellings where individual families of Ice Agers camped. Placing the floor of a dwelling a little below ground level helps keep out the cold.

northern Alaska used to crawl through a low tunnel that sloped down below ground level to the floor of their snow-block igloos. In the mountains of eastern Turkey and Armenia, among other places, much farther south but still bone-chilling in winter, country people have long built underground pit houses. Only the structure's roof remains exposed, with a hole to let fresh air in and smoke out.

Apparently Ice Agers learned this method of keeping out the cold many thousands of years ago. Besides the small holes in the ground where posts once stood, remains of many Ice Age campsites have shallow pits of various sizes and shapes. The size, numbers, and locations of these pits all have a story to tell. At a place in what is now Slovakia, in central Europe, two long pits extending 75 feet, connected by a short middle pit, form a sort of letter **H**, once the underground floor of what might be thought of as an Ice Age apartment house. Remains of seven separate hearths spaced near the edges indicate that a number of families lived there, perhaps under a

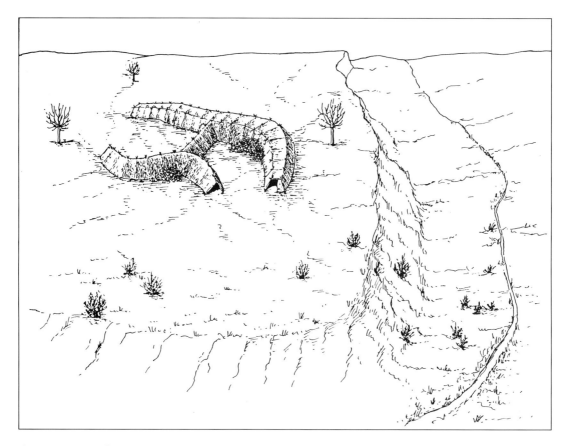

At a place in Slovakia, in eastern Europe, shallow trenches forming a long letter H, and the remains of seven hearths, suggest that a number of Ice Ager families shared a large, hide-covered "apartment house."

roof made of many hides. Other sites in the same region have several pits, each big enough for the floor of a one-family dwelling, where families lived within shouting distance of each other but not under the same roof.

In very cold places, the underground soil remains frozen all year round; only the top layer at the surface thaws during the warmer months. Digging pits 75 feet long and a foot or more deep in that dense, cold surface ground must have been quite a challenge for Ice Agers using stone tools. No doubt they had lots of energy and maybe a team of diggers working together.

Little pits often remain at the edges of a dwelling site. Some contained animal bones split to extract the marrow, suggesting that they served as trash bins. For Ice Agers, marrow supplied an important source of nutrition, and they probably liked the taste besides, as many of us do today. In the colder periods, pits like these could also be used for storing bones with meat on them until needed, a handy deep freezer within easy reach.

Other small pits held batches of stone tools, a sign that people who had camped for a season intended to return to the same place. We do that sort of thing today, locking up the summer house with its furniture and equipment until next year. And speaking of furniture, some Ice Age campsites include stone blocks, placed as if they could have been used as seats, perhaps covered with moss or hides to make them a bit softer—who knows?

But the biggest surprises in housing come from areas where living mammoths and the bones of mammoths long dead were common. Imagine collecting tons of mammoth bones, each one a challenge to move, dragging

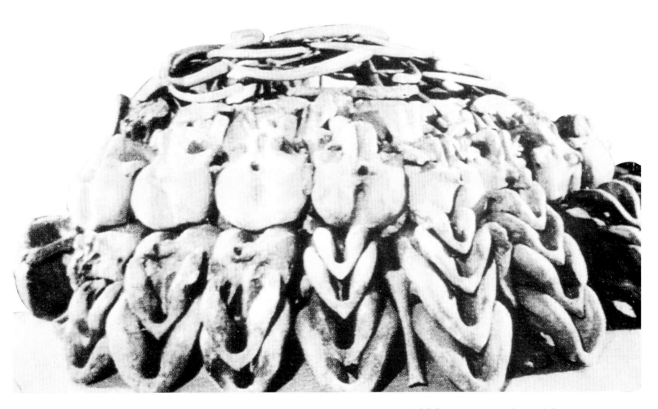

Ice Agers building shelters in the Ukraine grasslands 15,000 years ago found few trees but lots of mammoth bones. This amazing hut included hundreds of mammoth bones, from skulls to leg bones, with jawbones arranged to form a regular pattern in the wall.

them to the spot where you've decided to live, and piling them to make the walls of a large hut. Unlikely as it seems, Ice Agers did just that at a number of places.

At Mezhirich, north of the Black Sea, the remains of several such huts still exist. To build the biggest one, a round structure more than 20 feet across, Ice Agers used almost 400 bones of different mammoths. They included numerous skulls and an assortment of leg bones, pelvises, and shoulder blades. The roof, probably made of hide-covered branches, was held in place by tusks and, as a final flourish, two upright tusks framed the hut's entrance.

There's even more to this unexpected story. Examining the several mammoth-bone huts at Mezhirich, archeologists discovered that each one had walls made of bones chosen and arranged to create a particular pattern. For example, the builders of the biggest hut apparently set aside 95 jaw-bones, which they used to form a herringbone design in the wall. The Ice Agers who built these huts 12,000 years ago not only had the imagination—and the ingenuity—to use the best available building material, but their thinking went beyond the practical idea of shelter to a new realm of planning and artistry. In short, they invented architecture!

WHAT'S COOKING

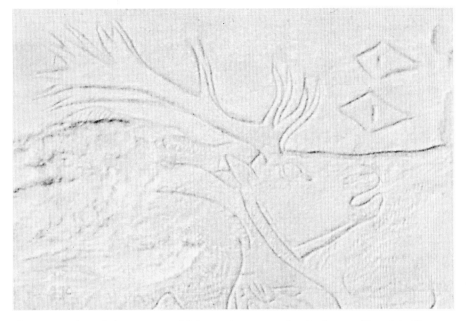

Compared with horses and bison, images of reindeer—like this fine engraved example from the Dordogne—are less common. But bones remaining at places where Ice Agers lived show that people ate a lot of reindeer meat.

WHETHER THEY CAMPED in rock shelters or mammoth-bone huts, life for Ice Agers often must have been no picnic. Hunting accidents, falls on the ice, or frostbitten nose or toes could always happen. And sometimes a cold period lasting years, with hardly a whiff of summer, could come on quickly and make things much worse: less choice of food, possibly even starvation. In those conditions, few kinds of plants can grow and many kinds of animals disappear.

But in better times, Ice Agers usually had plenty of animals to hunt, as if nature had provided a well-stocked supermarket on the hoof. The bones from a wide range of places make quite clear that they ate a variety of meat, with reindeer, horse, and bison most often heading the menus served up at their hearths.

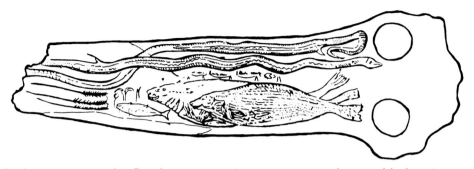

Seals that swam up the Dordogne rivers in summer may have added variety to Ice Agers' menus. This scene also shows snakes and plantlike forms—all possible menu items. Because the drawing was made by "unrolling" the engraving that surrounds a chunk of antler, a hole cut at one end of the antler appears as two holes.

That pattern holds true even at living sites in mammoth country. If you think about the dangers of hunting a mammoth, not to mention the work of cutting it into serving pieces, maybe that's no big surprise.

Fewer of the more delicate bones from small animals remain, but we can safely assume that menus also included species like hares, squirrels, and birds. Bones of the ptarmigan (a kind of grouse) have been found, for example, and ducks, geese, and other river birds would surely have been snared in season. Harpoon points and fishhooks from various Ice Age sites strongly suggest that Ice Agers caught salmon, which swim up rivers from the sea in the summer, and probably other fish, such as trout and pike. The seals that are pictured in certain Ice Age images must have come up the rivers too, perhaps following salmon, and could have been harpooned.

Where there are birds and fish, there are eggs. As archeologists have become more and more skillful at picking through the tiny bits and pieces they unearth and carefully sift, they have even sorted out scraps of eggshell. Salmon eggs, sometimes called red caviar, leave no shell behind but certainly could have been relished along with the salmon. Frogs' legs and snails may also have been delicacies in France during the Ice Age, as they are today. Maybe eating snails doesn't appeal to you, but tastes differ.

For Eskimos living in the far north, where conditions rule out most plants, animal foods used to tell just about the whole story of dinner. Ice

Large numbers of salmon may have swum up rivers of the Dordogne in summer, returning from the sea to spawn. Ice Agers could easily have speared them. This stone slab with its large sculptured salmon comes from a rock shelter ceiling.

Age temperatures often dropped as low as those in far northern regions do now, but there was an important difference. As you travel south, moving away from the top of the world and closer to the equator, the sun hits the Earth at a different angle and provides more warmth and a longer growing season. That gives plants a much better chance of getting on in life. Our Ice Agers living in the Dordogne probably had a fair variety of plant foods to choose from, especially in the warmer periods.

Although they can't move around like migrating birds or reindeer, plants come and go in their own way with the changing seasons. Trees that lose

their leaves as winter approaches grow new leaves when more sunlight and warmer days come again. Small leafy plants die down and return in spring or summer. And like animals, different plants need different conditions. You won't find crocodiles or palm trees in chilly places.

Unlike animals, however, plants have no bones or shells to leave behind. Many do leave seeds or tiny grains of pollen that can be identified if found, but seeds tend to disappear and pollen does not usually turn up at the places where people ate dinner. Though it's hard to tell exactly which plants Ice Agers might have eaten, we do know that people who live on what their local countryside provides soon learn which plants in the meadows and woods have fruits, roots, or other parts that are good to eat and where and when to find them. They also know which plants should be avoided. News of a bad mushroom that killed a neighbor or cousin gets around quickly.

As the seasons passed, Ice Agers undoubtedly encountered some mushrooms, good and bad—maybe even truffles. There were also acorns, probably flowering plants like dandelions and mustard with leaves to be used like salad greens, and, in marshy places, cattails with underground tubers to eat the way we eat potatoes. The Ice Age climate did not support large trees bearing fruits like apples or walnuts, but at the right times blackberries or strawberries and possibly hazelnuts may have grown in some places too. We can imagine a small group of sharp-eyed women and young children, like mushroom hunters today, walking along and filling their hide pouches with the best of whatever the season had to offer. While they were at it, they would have collected birds' eggs and snails.

Lots of plant foods are at their best eaten raw, the fresher the better. But most people think that meat becomes tastier and easier to eat when cooked. Some of the bones and stones from campsites suggest that once Ice Agers had their meat in hand, they did indeed cook it. For example, a raw bone can be split lengthwise without too much trouble, but it is much easier

Plants appear on this knife blade along with a bison head. Though traces of plants are harder to find than animal bones, we can be quite sure that Ice Agers gathered and ate leaves, berries, and roots in season.

to split or cut a bone crosswise with tools used by Ice Agers when the bone is cooked. At dwelling sites, bones charred at the ends and stones reddened or fractured by the heat of the fire likewise indicate that cooks have been at work. Whether the bones and stones are found in or near the hearth and how they are arranged count, too.

Chef's specials probably didn't include reindeerburgers, as chopping raw meat fine would have been difficult with the tools at hand, but tasty barbecued venison may well have been served up to the people gathered around the hearth. As you probably may have discovered on a camping trip or in your own backyard, to barbecue meat without burning it, you need to raise it above the fire. Another use for mammoth bones! At a number of campsites in mammoth country, Ice Agers had placed a pair of long, straight mammoth bones, or sometimes tusks, at opposite sides of the hearth, probably to support and raise the ends of skewers holding meat. In other regions, a pair of stone blocks seems to have served the same purpose. Skewers could have been made from a thin length of freshly cut branch, well sharpened at one end. It would be interesting to know whether men or women did the barbecuing.

Ice Agers built hearths to hold fires for warmth and cooking. In this drawing of a hearth found at a place in northwestern Siberia, stones in the middle could have been heated by the fire and used as griddles to broil meat or fish.

Ice Age cooks could also have preheated a stone slab for use as a grill either by setting it directly on the fire or by building a fire on top and removing the embers before placing meat or fish on the slab. Or they could have piled up small stones, heated the pile, and placed the food to be cooked in the middle. At a rock shelter in France, a little heap of ptarmigan bones lay amid small stones, once piled that way, which had been fractured by heat.

Clues point to still another cooking method, possibly the ancestor of the New England clambake or Hawaiian luau. Stones lining some of the little pits at the edges of places where Ice Agers lived show cracks and a reddened surface—signs of burning. Here's what could have happened: Line a shallow pit with stones, build a fire in the bottom, and let it burn down to embers. Now cover the fire first with a thin layer of something like damp leaves or grass, then your meat, wrapped in more leaves, then a layer of earth. The earth keeps the heat from escaping, so that the embers and the heated stones lining the pit will cook the meat.

Ice Agers may also have cooked some of their food in boiling water. That process can begin by filling a small pit with water, heating stones red hot in a big fire, and dumping them into the water. The stones can be heated in a fire right beside the water-filled pit and tumbled in at strategic intervals to keep the water boiling. Experiments to find out whether this method works showed that a red-hot stone about a foot long and six inches wide would make more than 100 gallons of water boil for 15 minutes. That's a lot of water, and the less water used, the fewer red-hot stones are needed to heat it.

It's fair to assume that people who could make well-sewn hide clothing could also make leakproof hide bags or buckets for carrying and perhaps storing water from a nearby stream or river. Even better, the hide bucket could become a cooking pot by throwing small heated stones into the water it contained.

Ice Agers may well have had such cooking pots. People living close to the seashore of northern Spain ate a lot of periwinkles, a small snail still popular in England. But periwinkles present a problem: their meat can't be removed from the shell unless you cook them. The many periwinkle shells found where these Ice Agers lived show no signs of having been put in or near the fire, however. The little periwinkles were probably cooked in some kind of container, using heated stones to boil the water. Many small stones found around the hearths show fractures or reddening that would have resulted from using them this way.

With pots, of course, we're dealing once again with materials that don't last. Ice Agers had no metal or pottery, but they could have made pots not only of hide, but of wood or bark, as some later peoples have done, possibly even coating some of them with clay. Such a pot could be hung over embers, so that the fire's heat would help the boiling without burning up the pot. Or the pot could be set on the ground nearby, depending on the hot stones to do the whole job. The French Ice Age specialist André Leroi-Gourhan, who examined many rock shelters in France, reported that the floors of a few had small circles of bare rock where such containers might have stood.

Add up all the guesses, some of them quite convincing, and you have grilling, roasting, baking, and boiling, most of the basic cooking methods we use today. It would seem that in good times, at least, Ice Agers could have enjoyed a full menu—all but gooey desserts. The Ice Age teeth that have been examined show no cavities. Luckily or unluckily, depending on how you look at it, that points to a lack of sweets.

TOOLS: MORE AND BETTER

LIKE SOME EVEN earlier humans, the Neanderthals who dominated the scene before our Ice Agers took over had two types of wooden spears: the kind that they sharpened at one end to thrust into an animal from up close and the kind, thrown from a distance, that was tapered at both ends for better balance as it zoomed through the air. A few of their spears have survived, including one stuck into the side of a mammoth.

These hefty Neanderthal hunters may have looked scary to their nineteenth-century discoverers, but they had some good, new ideas. For example, they were the first to think of attaching a stone spear point to a wooden shaft, making the spear more effective than the sharpened all-wood type. But they made their stone spear points mainly for attaching to their thrusting spears. We know this because the stone spear points for a spear to be thrown needed a narrower shape than the spear points for a spear to be thrust. Air resistance is one reason for that. Along came the Ice Agers and things changed. From about 40,000 years ago, when they appeared in western Europe, lots of narrow stone spear points suddenly begin to turn up at places where these new people lived and hunted. Apparently they realized more clearly than the Neanderthals did how much a more effective thrown spear could improve the chances of catching a large animal, such as a horse or an aurochs that hunters might not be able to approach.

Typically, when Ice Agers got hold of a good new idea, they worked to make it even better. As time passed, they kept on improving the shape and sharpness of their spear points. The spear-thrower, invented about 20,000 years ago, carried the success of throwing a spear a big step further. Some slim needlelike objects that could be stone arrow points, from about 3,000 years later, make some people think that Ice Agers also invented the bow and arrow. That question still awaits an answer, but evidence shows that they also made elegant barbed bone harpoons, another new throwing tool, well before the Ice Age ended.

The changes Ice Agers made to improve their tools went far beyond spears and other hunting weapons. Throughout the 25,000 years when they camped in places from Spain to Siberia, they proved to be masters of using, making, and inventing new and better tools for whatever they needed to do, from sewing clothes to engraving some of their famous animal images.

Like many another project, shaping a stone tool is easy if you know how. To do the job right requires choosing the proper kind and size of stone, holding the stone and the pounder at the proper angles, and knowing where and how to pound, or strike, to chip off pieces in the desired way. It's quite likely that young Ice Agers learned the knack of chipping stone in the same spirit in which people now become computer whizzes early in life.

Judging from more recent hunting societies, this kind of toolmaking was probably a job for men. But baskets, pouches, and pots are tools, too, usually made by women. We think that Ice Agers used such things, but no examples remain to give us details about how they might have been made.

Every man may have made his own stone tools, with perhaps a bit of extra help from a specialist for tricky finishing touches. Bits of chipped stone found clustered in some of the places where Ice Agers camped suggest that toolmakers used one part of the shelter as their workshop, a tidier plan than scattering stone chips over the whole shelter floor. No doubt making tools took up quite a lot of time, maybe during periods unsuitable for hunting, and as with toasters, radios, and much of our other equipment today, it was often easier to make a new tool than to repair a damaged one.

Stone tools can be shaped either by chipping down the main piece of stone, known as the core, or from the chunks chipped from it. In the language of stone toolmaking, even a large chunk removed from a core is called a flake.

To make stone tools like knives or chisels, Ice Agers first struck bits off a chunk of flint to flatten one side. Then they knocked against the edges of the flat side to chip off long flakes that could be shaped by further clippings.

Making stone tools may look easy, but it takes practice and skill to strike a piece of stone in the right places to shape the tool you have in mind. Here artist Pierre Laurent imagines an Ice Age toolmaker at work.

Flint, which forms lumps in a type of rock called limestone (the stuff caves are made of), was a favored material for stone toolmaking long before Ice Ager times. Because it is hard and glassy, it can be shaped by hammering to take a good sharp edge. But to break off neat flakes rather than shattering the flint, it needs to be hammered with a softer stone, or better yet the end of a sturdy branch or a piece of bone, such as a leg bone with a rounded end. Those softer materials also serve well for other jobs like breaking open snail shells or splitting bones to get at the marrow inside.

Ice Agers brought two big ideas to the age-old process of toolmaking. One was a new method for shaping tools more precisely. By pressing against a flint core with the edge of a small, flat-ended stone rather than striking it with a hammer, a toolmaker could remove smaller flakes. These flakes could then be shaped into more delicate, convenient tools for jobs such as piercing or cutting. Pressing off small bits from the flakes themselves could also sharpen a stone blade or spear point to a finer edge.

Ice Agers didn't invent the other idea, but they developed it to a fine art. This approach involves shaping a big piece of flint, maybe about the size of a football, to give it a flat top so that knocking against the rim with a stone or bone hammer will remove long, narrow flakes with parallel edges. These flat, blade-shaped pieces could be sharpened on one or both edges to become tools ranging from daggerlike knives to blunt-backed chisels.

Having a choice of blades makes a big difference. Even at dinner, we use one kind of knife to carve the roast, another to spread butter or cheese on bread, and a third type to peel an apple. Ice Agers had no butter or apples, but they did have plenty of meat and needed different kinds of blades to skin an animal and to cut it up, for example. We can tell that blades were often attached to a handle, probably using a sticky substance like pine sap to glue one end into a slotted piece of branch or by tying it onto a handle with thongs. As many of us know from experience, for most purposes a knife with a handle is easier to use than a knife blade without one.

The blunt-backed chisel, also known as a burin, brought another great change. A flint knife isn't strong enough to cut into bone—it will break first. But a stone burin is different. The user can press on the thicker, blunt edge to make the corner of the sharpened edge cut a groove in a piece of bone. Cut two such grooves parallel to each other and a strip of bone can be detached, opening the way to making a variety of other tools. And in the hands of Ice Age artists, the burin became an engraving tool to create images and patterns in objects made of bone. Reindeer antler and ivory

A stone chisel with a sharp corner can cut strips from a bone to shape it or, in the hands of an artist, create an engraved animal or other decoration in the surface.

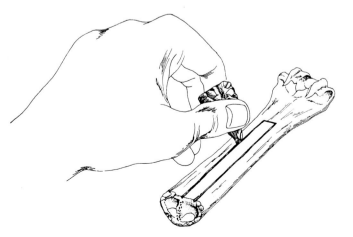

Ice Agers had the new idea of using bone and antler to make tools. These materials, less rigid than stone, can be precisely shaped to make a harpoon with little barbs or a needle with an eye.

from mammoth tusks can be shaped in the same way, and the term "bone tools" usually includes these materials.

People living in places like southwestern France, with its milder winters and valleys where some trees could grow, had wood to make spears and tools for hammering, digging, and other purposes. But north and east, on the cold, open plain, there were few trees. Lacking wood, Ice Agers living there led the way in making tools from bone and similar materials.

With reindeer that shed their antlers every year and dead mammoths whose tusks remain, lots of these materials could be found in one spot or another. And they offered some big advantages. For instance, people could use a sliver of stone to make a piercer that would punch a hole—but with bone, antler, or tusk they could make a needle with an eye. Likewise, they could make a stone spear point, but with bone they could make a harpoon point with delicately shaped barbs, or a curved fishhook. Even when it came to spear points, a bone point took a sharper edge than a stone point and didn't break as easily. Another limitation of stone: it can be made into some kinds of very small tools but very large ones would be too heavy and unwieldy. A long piece of reindeer antler is much handier to use for a job like digging, pointed side down.

It's easy to look back now and see how the changes that Ice Agers made—new materials, new kinds of tools, new ways to make them— provided more choices about how to do things and more successes in doing them. But changes really depend on looking forward. The people who bring them about have to imagine, before they can know, that experimenting with a new idea can make a difference. Look around at the TV antennas sprouting from every rooftop, the computers roosting on every desktop, and the airplanes zipping through the sky. These things were unknown only a century ago. The same kind of imagination that inspired these recent inventions and changed our lives was at work thousands of years ago when Ice Agers began improving their spears.

ART: A WHOLE NEW WORLD

CREATING IMPROVED TOOLS, such as a better spear or a needle, gave Ice Agers new ways to make life more successful from day to day. Creating art gave them something much more amazing. The world of images, never known before, provided a new way to express how they saw the real world they lived in and what it meant to them. The first Ice Age artists had made a profound discovery.

The beginnings of art remain a mystery. Eskimo artists, whose tradition as skillful, imaginative carvers goes back many centuries, say that the image they create is trapped in the piece of stone or ivory all along and they simply work to release it.

Maybe the first artists were inspired to try their hand at creating an image when the natural form of a stone, a lump of clay, or even a cloud suddenly reminded them of a familiar shape—a fish or a bird or even a horse. That's just a guess, of course.

Whatever the explanation may be, all of a sudden there was art, bursting forth in full glory. A few items, such as a simply shaped pendant or objects marked with lines, survive from Neanderthal times but no actual images. And then come the oldest examples of full-fledged art we know, a group of tiny ivory carvings from Vogelherd, in southeastern Germany, that go back more than 30,000 years. For artists to shape this elegant two-inch ivory horse, mammoth, and other figures so expertly, it seems that a learning period must have gone before—maybe modeling figures in a softer material such as clay, which allows for correcting mistakes, or carving them in wood. But if such examples ever existed, they vanished long ago.

Ice Agers took to their new-found art with the same energy that they took to improving their tools, and they kept on producing masterpieces for 20,000 years. Nothing escaped the keen eyes and sure hands of the artists as they created their likenesses of the animals around them. They pictured the heavy coat of hair that a horse grows in winter and the patchy look of a bison in summer when it sheds its winter coat. They captured the graceful curve of the lion's back, the compact build of the humped mammoth, and the delicate strength of the legs under a bull's bulky body. And they showed how the heavy bull differs from the smaller cow and the wobbly, long-legged calf.

To set down in strong, simple lines what you have observed so that a bison or a deer remains as real in your image as in life is a rare achievement. No group of more recent artists anywhere in the world have produced more powerful, vivid animal portraits than those the Ice Age artists created.

Were these first artists men or women or maybe both? The answer usually favors men, on the theory that hunters have time off, especially in bad winter weather, while we can guess that women's work was never done. When she wasn't out searching for plants, the Ice Age woman was busy making clothes, caring for children, and performing other daily duties.

To fit the shape of the antler spear-thrower it once decorated, an Ice Age artist created a carved bison with its head turned back. Details include the suggestion of a tongue, perhaps flicking away an annoying insect.

Male or female, Ice Age artists quickly figured out how to use or invent tools to portray animals in a great variety of ways. With their stone blades and chisels they could carve an image of a horse from a tiny piece of ivory or sculpt it, several feet long, on a rock face. The flat-backed stone chisel, or burin, that Ice Agers invented came in especially handy for engraving the image of a horse—or any other animal—by cutting lines into the surface of stone and other hard materials. Artists also knew how to use the bulges in a cave wall to give a painted animal a feeling of bulk. A wonderful example of how they also used the natural shape of a piece of antler to set an animal's form is a bison whose compact form neatly fits the shape of the spear-thrower it decorates: short legs, and the head turned back against its side as if to bite at an annoying insect.

For painting their animal scenes on cave walls, artists had brushes. Y'upik Eskimo artists living in the far north used paintbrushes made from squirrel tails to paint their masks. Ice Agers could surely have made something similar. A stiffer paintbrush can be made by chewing on the end of a twig to soften and fray it. Artists used their fingers, too, as can be seen in places like the French cave of Pech-Merle, where squiggly designs made in a soft clay ceiling were drawn this way. Certain caves also have images where the paint was sprayed, perhaps by blowing it through a hollow bird bone.

Ice Agers made their paint from a soft claylike mineral called ocher, which has a natural yellowish or red color. Traces of these colors remain on hollowed stones probably used to hold a lump of ocher, which would have been pounded to a powder with another stone and perhaps mixed with some material to modify the color. Stirring either water or animal grease into the powder made a moist mixture for painting. These two mixtures were the earliest forms of watercolor and oil paints. Recent experiments suggest that the water-mixed paint was best for sticking to rock walls. Charcoal—partly burned wood—served mainly for black outlines and shading.

To decorate cave walls, far from the light of day, you need not only paint, brushes, and engraving tools, but enough light to see what you are doing. You might also need something like a ladder or a scaffold for painting the upper part of the wall. There is good evidence that, as usual, Ice Agers knew what to do next. In the magnificent cave of Lascaux, a number of flat stone lamps remained, each nicely shaped with a hollowed-out center to hold the animal fat that probably served as fuel. Because the walls of Lascaux show no smoke smudges, we think that the wick placed in the fat was made of juniper bush wood or dried moss, which produce no smoke as they burn. As for a scaffold for artists to stand on, small holes bored into a few of the cave's walls could have been used for securing pegs for such a structure, made of branches and held together

To provide the needed light as they painted cave walls, Ice Age artists used stone lamps like this one found in the cave of Lascaux. They probably burned animal fat to light a wick made of dried moss or a strip of wood or bark.

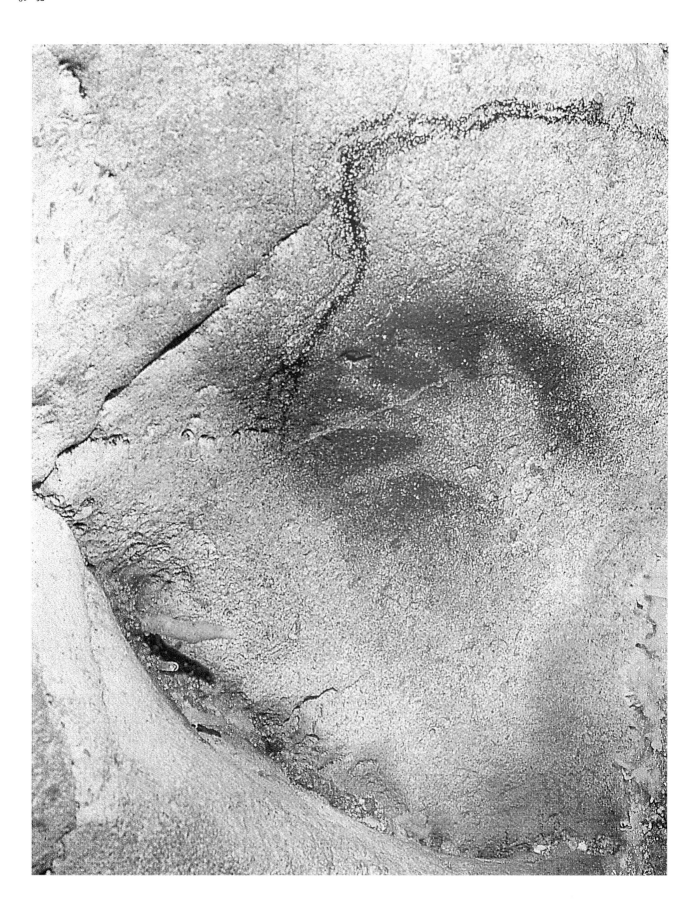

by rope. Astonishingly, like a footprint left forever in a clay floor, there is actually an imprint of a piece of rope, showing its twist.

Many of the cave floors do have footprints, too, some left by young children. At one time or another, nearly everybody must have made their way through the dark, twisting cave passages to join in whatever events happened in the special, decorated chambers. In some caves, people purposely left handprints, large and small. It seems that both adults and children held one hand against a cave wall while paint was sprayed around it, outlining the hand's shape. Leaving a handprint is like a writing a name in a visitors' book: it certainly proves that a particular person came there, but we don't know for what purpose. To make matters more mysterious, some of these handprints are missing a part of a finger.

Not every mystery can be explained, but of one thing we can be certain: Ice Agers didn't leave handprints deep in caves just for the fun of it or paint animals on the walls just for decoration. Like spoken words, art sends messages easily grasped by the people who understand that language. And again like words, different groups of people have different art languages. For some people, the picture of a person with wings and a halo immediately says "angel"; for others, the meaning of a winged person with a disk floating over the head may be as mysterious as an Ice Age handprint missing a finger is for us.

A quick march through art history shows that people the world over have made images of what looms large in their lives, both what they see and what cannot be seen. The angels, gods, and other invisible spirits that appear in various peoples' art are as real in their own way, and as important, to the people who make those images and look at them as the animals, trees, and people nearby.

People placed a hand against a cave wall, and paint was sprayed around it, maybe through a hollow bird bone, outlining the hand. Some of the handprints in Gargas, a cave in the French Pyrenees region, have parts of fingers missing. Nobody knows the reason why.

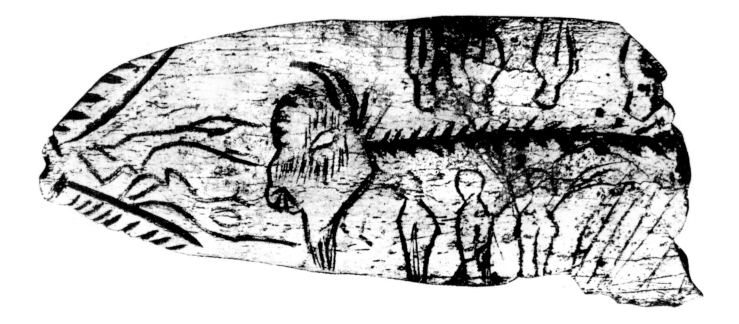

Like people who came later, Ice Agers could have linked some of their art with stories they told. This bone pendant engraved with a bison head and spine flanked by stylized human figures might well be an example.

Many peoples who live close to nature believe that all animals, trees, and sometimes winds, waters, and thunder have a spirit. People who live by killing animals for food and other needs have deep respect for these animals and consider their spirits very powerful. For example, Indians living on America's northwest coast relied on the consent of animal spirits for success in hunting. They also linked animal figures with their ancient ancestors and with some of their explanations of how basic things happen in nature. One story tells how daylight first came to the sky when Raven, a mischievous spirit, tricked the keeper of a box where the sun was locked up into letting him carry away the box so that he could let the sun escape.

Anyone can appreciate the beautifully stylized ravens, whales, and other animal forms that appear on the masks and rattles, totem poles, and feast dishes created by northwest coast artists. But while members of the northwest coast tribes can understand them at a glance, their meaning often puzzles outsiders. To get the message you have to know the art language.

Of course we can't assume that Ice Agers had the same ideas as people who lived thousands of years later. But the widespread belief in animal spirits among hunting groups all over the world, and the importance of animals in Ice Age art, suggest that something along those lines may be possible. For all we know, an image of a bison might represent either an actual living bison or the bison as spirit. We can also be quite sure that people who have art have stories, too, about what matters in their lives, and some of the art may relate to those tales. If only we could sit at an Ice Age hearth and hear one of those stories told!

Ice Age art doesn't begin and end with animals. It also includes designs. Squiggles, rooflike shapes, grids, and lots of other patterns regularly appear on cave walls and on objects like tools. We shouldn't be too surprised. Modern life is knee-deep in symbolic designs: stars for excellence, arrows to point the way, the logos on your favorite shoes and car, the icons on your computer screen, the traffic signs on the road. As far back as we can look, people everywhere have used design language. No doubt Ice Agers started the trend.

Along with the many animal forms, designs from dots to shapes resembling houses or feathers appear on cave walls and small objects. Their meaning was probably as clear to Ice Agers as traffic arrows and computer icons are to us.

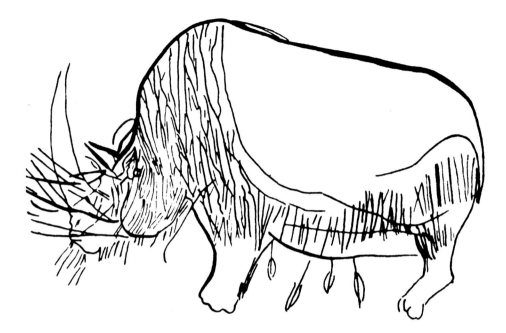

Few rhinoceros bones have been found in places where Ice Agers lived. The darts in the belly of the rhinoceros in this drawing, copied from an engraved stone, perhaps suggest the idea of killing this formidable beast rather than actually killing it.

Though we can't read the meanings of the Ice Agers' art language with any hope of real success, occasionally we get a tantalizing hint. Animal images include quite a few examples of horses and bison with marks on their bodies that look like spears. Maybe adding a spear mark to a horse or bison image was a way of "killing" it. Some of these marked animals also have an extra tail, horns, or legs, probably added at a later time. Perhaps adding a second tail created a new bison to be "killed" again during some repeated ceremony or other event. Maybe the idea was to inspire success in hunting. But maybe not. Strangely, there are almost no reindeer images marked this way, even though reindeer were the main source of meat. It looks as if a horse or bison image had an important meaning that went beyond the idea of providing food.

Ice Agers visiting caves left footprints by accident and handprints on purpose, but you have to look harder to find images of humans on cave walls. When they do appear, they may be rather abstract or have animal features. One such image, set high on a wall in the French cave of Trois Frères, pictures a man with a beard and antlers, the tail of a horse, and bear paws for hands. Depending on how you look at him, he may appear to be bent over in a dance or possibly crawling. Some people think that the reindeer head is a mask and that figures like this one may represent a shaman, a person believed to have special powers of communicating with spirits. Shamans have been important to many groups of hunters living in Siberia and the far north, among other places. Shaman or no, the figure is two feet long and must have had some special function.

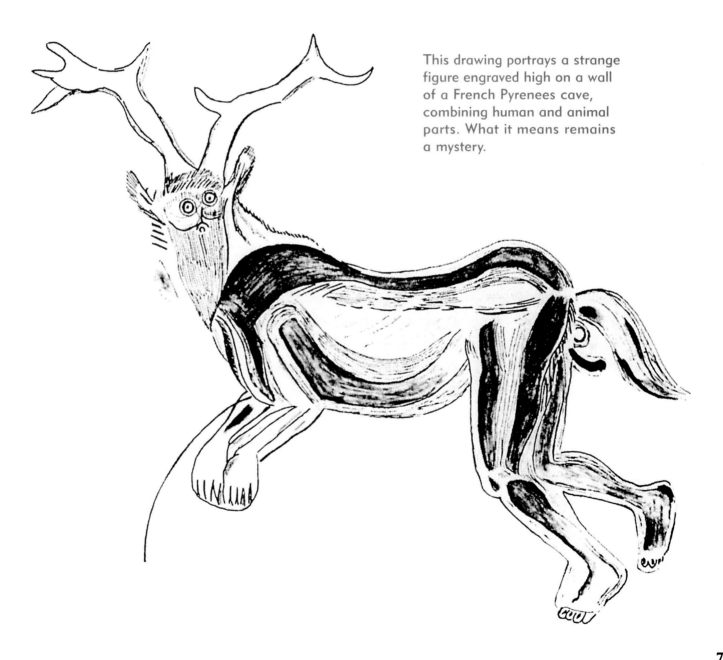

This drawing portrays a strange figure engraved high on a wall of a French Pyrenees cave, combining human and animal parts. What it means remains a mystery.

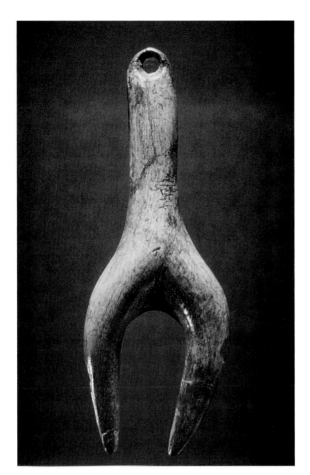

Art styles often grow more abstract over time. By the late Ice Age, an ivory "Venus" from a place in the Czech Republic had become an upper rod with curved tapering legs. But like earlier, more female-looking figures, it probably relates to the idea of fertility.

From caves and the world outside them come a series of striking carved female figures, some of which look as if they could be the work of a modern artist. The earliest example, from the site called Willendorf, in Austria, seems to have set the style for some of the many that followed. The sculptor shaped this small stone figure to bring out the uniquely female features of a woman's body. Short and round, she is mostly bulging middle, with puny little arms, footless legs tapering off to nothing, and a head that lacks a face. She does have bracelets and a fancy hairdo, though—proving that Ice Agers paid attention to such matters 30,000 years ago. Some people think that what looks like a hairdo may actually represent a cap woven from fiber. Over thousands of years, artists in many different

For thousands of years, Ice Agers sculpted female figures, many with exaggerated midsections and sketchy arms, legs and head. A very early example—30,000 years old—is this small figure, carved in limestone, from the site of Willendorf, in Austria.

places carved other such female figures in various materials and sizes, including quite a large one modeled on a chunk of rock. Some are tall, some more lifelike, others more abstract. But all are unmistakably female, and people now call them Venus figures, after the Roman goddess of love.

Clearly, these "Venuses" meant something special to Ice Agers. Women who look as pregnant as a number of these figures do will soon bring a new baby into the world. It's easy to connect them with the idea of new life. For example, some of the first farming peoples made similar figures, linked with the hope that their fields would produce good new crops. Ice Agers didn't farm, of course, but through these figures they might have been expressing hope for the bounty of nature: new plants coming up and new animals born each year. Or they could have been hoping for enough children to carry their group into the future, or even for a return to life in a new body after death. Another unsolved Ice Age puzzle.

All the Venuses from Europe are naked except for the occasional neckband or bracelet, but some of the little ivory females carved by artists in Malta, Siberia, seem to be wearing something like ski suits with marks on them suggesting fur. They are thinner than most of the western figures, too, with less attention given to female features. Maybe these Ice Agers lived too far away from other groups to pick up the same style. Uniquely, the artists in Malta also carved small ivory birds. Some more recent societies connect birds with flights of the spirit.

Now for the big surprise. Just when everybody thought that Ice Agers hardly ever pictured themselves, a treasure trove came to light. At the rock shelter of La Marche, the French archeologist Léon Pales discovered more than a hundred flat fist-sized stones engraved on both sides. Amidst a tangle of other lines, he deciphered human faces, bodies without heads, and whole figures.

Ice Age female figures, with bulging breasts, belly and buttocks, are often called Venuses, for the Roman goddess of love. The elegant little ivory "Venus of Lespugue," from southwestern France, fits the pattern.

Whoever made these sketches in stone had an eye for key details, like a good cartoonist. The faces, always in profile, have a variety of individual-looking noses, chins, and hairstyles. A few men have a neatly trimmed beard or mustache, but most do not. It seems that Ice Agers must have shaved, a smart idea in a climate where your beard might freeze on a brisk winter day. The full bodies include standing, sitting, and kneeling figures, several with arms raised as if in prayer. A few also wear headbands or jewelry such as bracelets, but in many cases, it's hard to tell whether the face or figure belongs to a woman or a man.

At last we get a glimpse of the real Ice Agers. Cavemen? Not on your life!

The tangle of lines on stones discovered at La Marche, a rock shelter in western France, have revealed many drawings of human faces and figures. This unique group of 15,000-year-old portraits gives us a hint of what Ice Agers looked like, including their hair styles.

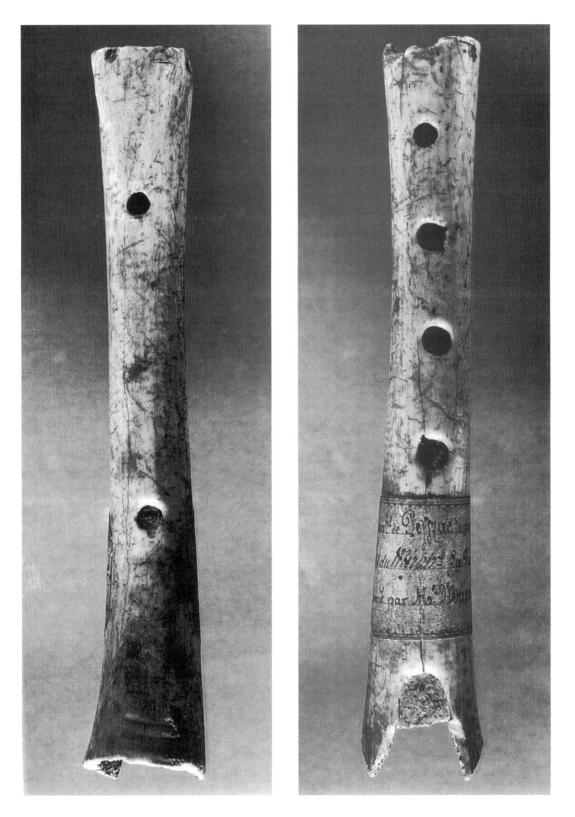

Besides creating art, Ice Agers performed music, as shown by this bone flute from the Dordogne. A group of twenty-thousand-year-old instruments, discovered in the Ukraine, includes various mammoth bones and an antler mallet to strike them, like a xylophone, to produce a range of tones.

BIBLIOGRAPHY

Avant les Scythes, préhistoire de l'art un URSS (exhibition catalogue). Paris: Ministère de la Culture at de la Communication, Editions de la Réunion des Musées Nationaux, 1979.

Bibikov, Sergei N. "A Stone Age Orchestra." *UNESCO Courier* (June 1945).

Chard, Chester H. *Man in Prehistory.* New York: McGraw Hill, 1975.

Coon, Carleton S. *The Hunting Peoples.* Boston: Little Brown, 1972.

Fitzhugh, William W. and Aron Crowell, eds. *Crossroads of Continents, Cultures of Siberia and Alaska* (exhibition catalogue). Washington, D.C.: Smithsonian Institution Press, 1988.

Hadingham, Evan. *Secrets of the Ice Age, The World of the Cave Artists.* New York: Walker & Co., 1979.

Leroi-Gourhan, André, director. *Les structures d'habitat au paléolithique supérieur.* Paris: Centre National de la Recherche Scientifique, 1976.

Lisitzky, Genevieve. *Four Ways of Being Human: An Introduction to Anthropology.* New York: Viking Press, 1956.

Lister, Adrian and Paul Bahn. *Mammoths.* New York: Macmillan, 1994.

Marshack, Alexander. *The Roots of Civilization.* Mt. Kisco: Moyer Bell, 1991.

Pales, Léon. *Les gravures de la Marche, II-Les Humains.* Paris: Ophyrs, 1976.

Perlès, Catherine. *Préhistoire de feu*. Paris: Masson, 1977.

Soffer, Olga and N. D. Praslov, eds. *From Kostenki to Clovis: Upper Paleolithic Paleo-Indian Adaptations*. New York: Plenum Press, 1993.

Spiess, Arthur E. *Reindeer and Caribou Hunters: An Archaeological Study*. New York: Academic Press, 1979.

Stoliar, A. D. "On the Sociohistorical Decoding of the Upper Paleolithic." Soviet Anthropology and Archaeology, fall 1997: Volume XVI, no. 2.

Tattersall, Ian. *Becoming Human: Evolution and Human Uniqueness*. New York: Harcourt Brace & Co., 1998.

White, Randall. *Dark Caves, Bright Visions* (exhibition catalogue). New York: American Museum of Natural History with W. W. Norton, 1986.

INDEX

Note: Page numbers in *italics* refer to illustrations

PHOTOGRAPH AND ILLUSTRATION CREDITS

Photographs and illustrations are courtesy of the following:

Alexander Marshack: pp. viii, 17, 18, 24, 31, 34, 39, 45 (both), 46, 47, 55, 56, 58, 70, 76, 77, 78, 81, 86

Douglas Maxonowicz: p. 20

American Museum of Natural History: pp. 13, 23, 26, 28, 33, 37, 38, 39, 41, 43, 48, 63, 68, 80, 82

Randall White: pp. 34, 57, 82, 83

after Léon Pales: pp. 22, 84, 85

Les structures d'habitat au paléothique supérieur: pp. 51, 52

Préhistoire de feu: p. 60

Pierre Laurent in *Unesco Courier.* Aug.–Sept. 1972: p. 66

after Peter Storck, in Chester H. Chard's *Man in Prehistory*: p. 40, 67

Jean Vertut: pp. 6, 15, 70, 72

Alexei Tikhonov: p. 27

O. N. Bader: p. 30

American Antiquity. Jan. 1985: p. 46

Archaeological Institute, Kiev, COUNTRY: p. 53

J. Oster, Musée de l'Homme, AMNH: p. 23

Musée des Antiquités Nationalies, AMNH: pp. 37, 39, 48, 72, 73

after Abbé Breuil, AMNH: p. 79

Robein Robert: p. 74

R. White: p. 68

Eugene Bergmann: p. 65